BAITED BREATH

FISH CAMP COZY MYSTERIES, BOOK 3

SUMMER PRESCOTT

SUMMER PRESCOTT BOOKS PUBLISHING

CHAPTER ONE

Eugenia Barkley sat on her couch with a soft, fawn-colored, handknitted throw over her pajama-clad legs, working on an article featuring ten ways to organize a living space. When she glanced up, loving the view of the lake outside the cabin's picture window, she was delighted to see a light snow falling. Sparkling flakes drifted down, blanketing the land around the lake in pristine white. It was magical. Eu smiled.

"Well, you definitely don't see this in Los Angeles," she murmured aloud.

Wrapping her hands around her favorite mug, she realized that the coffee she'd been drinking had gone cold as she'd become absorbed in writing, so she went to the kitchen to pour more of the piping hot brew into her cup, along with a dollop of heavy cream. It was an indulgence, but it somehow seemed to make the frosty scene outside the window far less chilly.

Eu had just sat down, and was smoothing the throw back over her legs, when her phone rang. Her best friend's face smiled up at her from the phone screen.

"Fran!" she exclaimed after hitting the answer button, eager to speak with her bestie. "Oh my gosh, it's snowing here and it's so beautiful. Partly because I haven't left the house yet," she said, chuckling.

"Hey, Eu! It's great to hear your voice. I can't even fathom snow right now. I probably won't even need a sweater to go outside today. So, how's life?" Fran asked.

"It's good. Pretty simple. I've been making sure I leave the house every day, either to go for a walk or go fishing, and I've had tons of quiet time to do my articles. How are you?"

"Lonely," Fran replied. "That's why I called. I absolutely cannot stomach the thought of Christmas without you, so I've made my reservations and I'll be there for a couple of weeks," she announced.

"Yay! Wait a minute young lady… are you sure you're not just avoiding your dad's invitation to go to Aspen with your stepmom's family?" Eu asked.

"That just provided a little extra incentive, but no. I miss you and the thought of you alone there and me alone here just made me crazy."

"No party invitations?" Eu's brows rose.

"Of course I have party invitations, but I'd rather be snowed in while visiting my bestie in the middle of nowhere." Fran laughed. "I'm closing the shop for a couple of weeks and heading your way."

They chatted for a few minutes longer, so that Eu could get the details of Fran's arrival time, then hung up. Eu couldn't even begin to wipe the silly grin from her face whenever she thought of Fran's visit. They'd have a little over two weeks of quality girl time, and she couldn't wait.

Buoyed by the news, Eu decided to get out of the house and do a bit of fishing before the accumulation of snow made it too annoying to walk from her cabin down the hill to the fishing hole and back. Since the cabin was on a peninsula, she loved having the option of using jerkbait to catch crappie or bass from her dock behind the cabin, or to use less conventional bait, like marshmallows, cheese, or even hotdogs, to catch catfish from the fishing hole located across the parking lot and down the hill from the front of her cabin.

Wrapping plastic shopping bags around her running shoes and tying them securely around her ankles because she forgot to buy boots for the season, she stepped carefully down the path to her dock to fish and brought in a couple of nice-sized crappie that would taste amazing sauteed in butter for her lunch. While solitude was nice, and the fish were biting, Eu craved human interaction and decided to head over to the fishing hole. Her sourpuss of a neighbor, Crappie Callie, rarely answered her attempts at conversation, but even being ignored was sometimes better than being alone, so Eu trudged down the hill with her basket of crappie, determined to kill her irascible neighbor, the only other person in the resort complex, with kindness.

“Good morning, Callie. Anything biting?”

Callie ignored her as usual, so Eu continued talking as she set up her pole and dropped her line down into the fishing hole.

"I know you don't like me for some reason, and that's okay. No one ever said we have to like everybody we meet. I just thought since we're the only two here this winter, it'd be nice to at least have a conversation."

No reaction, so Eu continued, sitting down in her chair, her breath making little white clouds when she spoke.

"I'll be out of your hair soon enough, I suppose. I've been here looking for more information about my mom. I never knew her. Never heard from her. Never even got a birthday card from her. I don't know what I could've done as a little kid to make her not want to talk to me, but it's kinda bugged me my whole life, you know? Anyway, if I don't find anything else before spring, I guess I'll just give up, even though I just have this feeling that there's more to her story than I know."

She thought she saw a flicker of something in Callie's face when she finished speaking, but a hard tug on her line prevented her from digging into what might have been behind it. She picked up her pole and started to reel, grunting with effort. Walking sideways along the side of the fishing hole to prevent the fish from diving beneath the decks and detaching itself, Eu worked the line, reeling with all of her strength, while desperately trying to keep the tip of her pole elevated so that the fish didn't unhook itself.

"Oh man, this feels like a good one," she blurted, her teeth clenched with effort.

Much to her surprise, Callie rose from her chair and grabbed the net, but she was too busy wrangling the determined fish to put too much thought into it.

"Whoa!" Eu exclaimed, when a large catfish broke the surface of the water, it's green and white side flashing briefly before it dove again. "It's huge!"

Callie, standing roughly three feet away, net hovering over the water, didn't reply, but was watching intently for Eu to bring the beast to the surface. Eu reeled, her hand aching, and saw a fin pop up. In one expert stroke, Callie plunged the net into the water below the fish and netted it, lifting it over the rail around the fishing hole and placing it gently on the deck, as far away from the edge of the water as possible.

"Wow, thanks," Eu said, breathing hard after the battle.

Callie nodded once, her face expressionless, and went back to her chair on the opposite side of the fishing hole.

Thrilled with her catch and her progress with Callie, Eu took the big catfish, along with her two crappie, to a cleaning station on a nearby dock, and was a bit crestfallen to discover that Callie was gone when she returned to the fishing hole. Still excited about her catch, she went back up to the cabin, thankful that a kindly local named Benz had taught her how to clean a catfish. After cutting the giant filets into more manageable chunks, she stuck them in the freezer and used one of the fresh crappie filets for a delicious early lunch.

As Eu was enjoying her food, she decided to text Benz to thank him again for his guidance when it came to catfish and was surprised when he responded with an invitation to a Christmas party.

"Oh, Fran will love that," Eu murmured with a grin.

She texted back to ask if she could bring a friend and, with the southern hospitality for which the area was famous, Benz agreed immediately, saying that he'd email her the invitation so she'd have all the details.

"We're going to a party," Eu said, doing a little happy dance while still holding her fork. "I can't wait to tell Fran!"

CHAPTER TWO

Eu's heart skipped a beat when she heard the crunch of tires on the snow in the parking lot as Fran's Uber pulled up in front of the cabin. While she was being quite productive and had discovered that she could survive a winter alone in the Ozarks, her heart overflowed at the reality of a visit from her best friend.

She had to laugh when Fran stepped out of the Uber, still flirting with the driver, dressed like a snow bunny in a light blue ski jacket, mittens, hat, and scarf. She tilted her face to the sky, grinning at the light snow that was falling.

Eu opened the cabin door and dashed out, only to be engulfed by an enormous hug from Fran, the faux fur edging on her bestie's coat tickling her cheek.

"It's so pretty here," Fran exclaimed. "The snow is amazing!"

Eu laughed. "Yeah, it's amazing until you have to stand out in it with your fingers freezing to clean a fish."

"Eww. Who even are you right now?" Fran wrinkled her nose. "Before you moved here the closest you ever got to cleaning a fish was eating dollar sushi on Thursdays."

Eu shook her head. "Ahhh the good old days. Let's get you inside. It's warm and there are baked goods."

The Uber driver had already placed Fran's extensive collection of bags on the porch, so she thanked him profusely, tipped him, and gave him a hug for good measure. For his part, the young man beamed as though he'd been given an early Christmas present.

Eu smiled, not for the first time, wishing that she had Fran's friendly finesse when it came to dealing with people.

"Are you moving in for the season?" Eu asked, laughing but halfway hoping.

"No ma'am, but I have definitely prepared for the Christmas season, and we're going to put up a tree and decorate it. The big suitcase has presents in it." Her eyes sparkled.

"I hope you tipped the driver well," Eu said, grabbing one of the larger suitcases and hauling it inside.

"Oh, I did. His name was Andrew, and he was so sweet – we had the best conversation," Fran replied, picking up the other massive suitcase and following Eu into the cabin.

"How do you even do that?" Eu asked, grunting as she set the suitcase down in the guest room. "You make friends with every single person you meet."

"Not everyone, as it turns out." Fran made a face. "Wait until I tell you about this insufferable woman on the plane."

"Can't wait. She must've been awful if YOU couldn't charm her. You can tell me all about it while we put together some homemade pizza. Michael made several crusts for me before he left, and I have a ton of toppings."

"Sounds delish. He really takes good care of you, doesn't he?" Fran waggled her eyebrows while taking off her coat.

"Oh, stop it, he's just a sweet person who loves helping people."

"Mmmhmmm…" Fran's tone was skeptical.

"Okay, if you want to go get unpacked and settled in, I'll get everything out for the pizza and start chopping the veggies, then we can make our own pizzas and get them baking," Eu said.

"Nice change of subject, bestie," Fran said over her shoulder as she headed down the hall. "But we'll explore that topic more later."

By the time Fran had stashed her clothing in the closet and dresser, Eu had finished chopping mushrooms, peppers, olives, tomatoes, and onions, and had precooked sausage crumbles, while the oven preheated.

"Oh, it smells amazing out here already," Fran announced, coming into the kitchen wearing yoga pants and a sweatshirt with a sasquatch on it, her hair tucked up into a messy bun.

The two friends stood side by side at the counter, with Fran sneaking pepperonis to munch on while they spread ingredients on their pizzas.

"So, spill it, what happened with the insufferable woman?" Eu asked, munching on a strip of green pepper.

"Well, by some miracle, I got upgraded to First Class, and I was so excited to see what it was like. So, I ordered a drink and food, and they brought out actual dishes and cloth napkins, it was amazing, but this older woman next to me was complaining about everything, and she wasn't quiet about it. I would've hated to be the flight attendant who had to deal with her. She was mad because her husband was sitting in front of her instead of beside her, but when I offered to trade places, he insisted that I keep my seat. I mean, I don't blame him, it was probably a nice break for him to get away from her," Fran explained, while placing pepperonis on her pizza, each round an exact distance away from the next.

"Couldn't you just put some earbuds in and pretend to go to sleep?" Eu asked, shuddering.

"Nope, she kept talking to me and complaining the whole time. So finally, we hit a bit of turbulence just as she was taking a drink of her mimosa, and it splattered down the front of her. I couldn't help myself; I snickered. It just slipped out and she went off like a rocket screeching about how I'd jostled her and then laughed about it. Not that I wasn't tempted, mind you, but I didn't do it. So it went on for a few minutes, and…" Fran sighed.

"And you went off on her," Eu said.

"Yeah, I'm not proud of it, but I did. I called her out on being rude to everyone and being negative about everything, and that if she lived her life that way, she was sure to be miserable, but it wasn't fair of her to inflict it on the rest of us. I think I saw her husband smirk a little when the rest of first class applauded."

Eu's mouth dropped open. "That's amazing." She grinned, proud of her friend for being brave enough to stand up to an obnoxious stranger.

"Yeah, it kinda was." Fran chuckled.

Eu slid their pizzas into the oven and set a timer on her phone.

"Well, I have some good news for you. We've been invited to a Christmas party," she announced.

Fran's eyes lit up. "Yay! Tell me all about it!"

"He said he was going to email me the invitation, so let me check the details," Eu replied, tapping at her phone. "Okay, here it is," she said, scanning the invitation. "Oh no."

"Oh no, what?" Fran asked, frowning and scooting closer to Eu to look at her phone.

"It's formal, and it's tomorrow. I don't even have office casual clothes here, never mind formal, and there's no way we can whip up an outfit in time," Eu lamented.

Fran rubbed her hands together with glee. "Challenge accepted," she said. "There's a thrift shop here that's still open, right?"

"Well, yes, but how's that going to help? This is a really ritzy party. We can't show up looking like the country cousins," Eu replied.

"And we won't. We'll find some dresses with great fabric and remake them. We'll show up looking like the couture cousins. You said there's a sewing machine here, right?" Fran asked.

“Yeah. I still can’t figure out why there’s one here, because from what I heard of my mom, she wasn’t exactly the Susie Homemaker type.”

Fran gazed at Eu for a moment. “Not everything is always as it seems. Now, let’s eat our lunch and head for the thrift store. This is going to be fun. And if there are snooty people who don’t appreciate our amazing dresses, that’s their problem.”

“Oh, boy. Okay, then. But what about like shoes and jewelry and all of that?” Eu fretted.

“We’re just going to have to get creative.” Fran’s eyes sparkled.

CHAPTER THREE

“So, did you buy this car?” Fran asked, easing into the passenger seat of Michael’s sedan.

“No, it’s Michael’s,” Eu replied, entirely unable to keep the blush from rising in her cheeks.

“He gave you a car?” Fran’s eyes went wide.

“No, of course not. He just left it here for me to use over the winter. I guess he has another one at home, and he didn’t want me to be stranded.” Eu shrugged.

“Wow, that’s mighty generous from a man who has absolutely no interest in you,” Fran teased.

“He’s just a really nice guy who likes to help people,” Eu replied, feeling her blush darkening.

“Yeah, and I’m sure that has nothing to do with the fact that you’re a smart, attractive, and capable woman.” Fran gave her a pointed look.

“First of all, thank you for trying to stoke my ego, and secondly, no, it doesn’t. I’m sure he’d do the same for Crappie Callie if she needed it.”

“How was his visit when he surprised you?” Fran asked.

“It was fun. We played games and fished, and he baked a ton to stock my freezer. I was sad to see him go, but that doesn’t in any way mean that he felt the same about me.”

“Okay, Debbie Denial.” Fran laughed.

Eu was spared from continuing the conversation when they pulled up in front of the thrift shop.

There was a section of gowns that was surprisingly large.

“Well, even in the Ozarks, girls go to prom and bridesmaids donate their dresses,” Fran remarked. “Now, let’s find some beauties to remake.”

Fran found a fuchsia satin gown that she felt she could makeover, and Eu found a sparkly gold gown with tulle accents. When they looked at accessories, they each found small evening bags that they could decorate with scraps of fabric from their dresses, and Fran, much to Eu's consternation, grabbed a handful of beaded necklaces with the goal of making earrings, bracelets, and maybe even new necklaces.

"Okay, now, shoes," Fran said, dragging Eu along behind her. They stopped on their way when Eu spotted two faux fur capes that they could wear over their dresses, then continued on to the shoes. They each found a pair of strappy heels that were entirely the wrong color, and Eu was confused when Fran put them in the cart.

"We can't possibly wear those with our dresses. They don't match in any way," she protested.

"Is there a hardware store that's still open?" Fran asked.

"Yeah, I think so. Why?"

"With a little bit of spray paint, we'll have shoes that match our dresses in no time," Fran replied.

"Please tell me you're kidding," Eu gasped.

"Would you rather wear jogging shoes with your dress?" Fran asked sweetly.

"Fine. We'll go to the hardware store, but if it doesn't work out, I'm not going," Eu warned.

"You're going," Fran said.

The two besties came back to the cabin, their arms laden with shopping bags. The goal was to create appropriate formal dresses. Eu was skeptical, and Fran was delighted. They each tried on their dresses and laughed when they saw each other. Both gowns hung from them like bad drapes.

"I think mine will be okay if we just take in the shoulders a bit so that it doesn't fall off," Eu observed, gazing at her reflection in the full length mirror in her walk-in closet.

"Oh, heck no, honey. We're taking yards of material out of this thing and showing off that Betty Boop shape of yours," Fran replied, hands on her hips.

"I'm not crazy about that idea," Eu replied, smoothing the fabric over her hips.

"No, you're just crazy," Fran teased. "If you've got it, flaunt it, Eugenia. I plan to." She gathered a handful of fabric behind her back to change the silhouette of her dress, and of course, looked amazing. Years of surfing in southern California had been kind to Fran.

"We may have a problem though," Eu said, gazing wistfully in the mirror.

"A problem? What?" Fran's brows rose.

"I passed sewing when I took Home Economics, but I haven't been near a sewing machine since."

Fran shrugged. "I've sewn up a few things over the years, we'll figure it out. How hard can it be? You just stand still while I pin some things together and we'll go from there."

"We're going to embarrass ourselves," Eu predicted.

"Not a chance. It doesn't matter what you wear, just step into the place like you own it and you'll be fine," Fran replied, opening the box of pins.

She made swags of fabric which clung to Eu in all the right places without being too tight or overly revealing. By the time Fran was done with the golden dress at the sewing machine, it looked like a designer original.

"Wow," Eu breathed, her mouth dropping open. "How did you do this? It's amazing!"

"Thanks! Honestly, I love watching that Next in Fashion show where all of these designers compete, and I've been practicing at home," Fran admitted.

"Really? I love that! You never cease to amaze me, girl." Eu grinned.

"Sometimes I amaze myself." Fran laughed. "Now it's my turn, but I'm going to need your help. I'll tell you where to put the pins, and you just put them in without stabbing me, deal?"

"I'll try my best." Eu laughed.

Fran's dress, while a bit more revealing, came out just as stunning as Eu's, and she did a little happy dance when she saw herself in the mirror.

"Okay, now that the hard part is done, do you want to make jewelry or spray paint the shoes?" she asked.

Eu made a face. "Neither?"

Fran folded her arms and gave her a look.

"Fine. I'll play with the jewelry – you do the shoes."

"Good. Don't forget, we can always use some of the spray paint on the jewelry too if we need to," Fran replied, digging in Eu's stash of packing paper to lay out a surface that would protect the flooring from spray paint.

"Ugh," Eu replied. She took the pieces that they'd bought at the thrift store and chose the ones that looked the most expensive. "Okay, if I cut these apart and use the crystal beads with the fuchsia glass beads, it'll look amazing with your dress. Then, if I take the rest of the crystal beads and string them on this thin gold chain, it should work with my dress. I have gold earrings that I can wear, and we can make fuchsia glass earrings for you, then we can make big chunky bracelets out of this big gold chain link necklace."

"Now you're talking," Fran said, already bending over and spritzing the shoes with gold paint. "Get to it, girl, and don't forget to make some kind of fancy thing for the faux fur capes closures."

"Sure... In my spare time," Eu groused, secretly enjoying the thought.

The two chatted while they worked, and time flew by. By the time all of the pieces of their outfits were complete, the sun had gone down and they were both starving.

"Let's do our final reveal after dinner," Eu suggested. "I need food."

"Same." Fran nodded. "What are we fixing?"

"I'm thinking comfort food. How do you feel about chili dogs and mac n cheese?" Eu asked.

"I'm totally on board."

They cooked together, with Fran catching Eu up on what had been happening with all their friends in L.A. during her absence, and Eu entertained Fran with tales of her adventures in the Ozarks. After having their fill of what they declared to be the world's best chili dogs and mac n cheese, and doing the dishes, they sank back into the couch to relax a bit before trying on their outfits.

"How do you get anything done? I could stare out of this window, watching the snow falling in the glow of your deck lights forever," Fran mused.

“Yeah, it is pretty magical around here,” Eu agreed.

“Ready to try on your outfit?” Fran asked.

“Accessories and all?” Eu clarified.

“Of course.”

“Let’s do it.”

The two emerged from their rooms fully dressed and met in the living room.

“You look amazing!” they said in unison, laughing afterwards. They hurried back to Eu’s room to preen in front of the full-length mirror.

“We’re probably going to stand out like sore thumbs among all of those rich people,” Eu said, smoothing the mink-colored faux fur of her cape.

Fran held her hair up and turned from side to side to see her necklace and earrings. “Nah, we’ll be trend-setters.”

“Should we be responsible and go to bed early tonight because we’re going to be up late tomorrow?” Eu asked, unhooking her cape and necklace.

“Heck no, lady! I’m only going to be here for a couple of weeks – we need to make the most of our time together," Fran replied.

"Agreed. I have a bottle of wine with our names on it, and we can watch some silly rom coms."

"With cookies?" Fran asked hopefully.

"That's a given," Eu replied.

CHAPTER FOUR

Eu was up and had made it halfway through her first cup of coffee when Fran wandered out to the dining room yawning and rubbing her eyes.

"I always sleep so well when I'm here," she said, gazing out the window at the lake.

"I'm glad, sleepyhead. Are you ready for coffee and muffins?" Eu asked, rising.

"Yes but sit down. I'll help myself. We lived together, remember? You don't have to wait on me while I'm here," Fran replied with a smile.

They sat quietly, munching on muffins and washing them down with coffee while they both woke up a bit, then decided to go for a morning walk to clear their heads.

“So, this is what fresh air smells like,” Fran said, stepping out onto the front porch and drawing in a deep breath.

“Yeah, it’s pretty great. I haven’t been here long enough to take it for granted,” Eu replied. “It still takes my breath away when I look at the lake and the trees. It’s so beautiful.”

“Are you changing your mind about leaving?” Fran asked.

“No. I’m still just determined to find out more about my mom before I go.”

“Then what?”

“Good question. Want to walk down to the fishing hole?”

“Oh, that’d be great,” Fran replied. “Hopefully Callie will be there.”

“Hooray,” Eu said tonelessly.

They carefully made their way down the path to the fishing hole.

"Aw, man. She's not here," Fran said when she saw Callie's chair was empty. "I wanted to catch up."

"Life's full of disappointments." Eu chuckled.

Fran nudged her with an elbow and gave her a reproving look.

"Want to stick around and see if I can catch anything since we're here?" Eu asked.

"Yep. With any luck, Callie will come down and you'll have a chance to be nice to her." Fran arched an eyebrow.

"I'll look forward to that."

Eu dropped a line into the water, and they waited, watching for a bite. And waited. And waited.

"I don't think there are any more fish left in there," Fran said.

"You may be right," Eu replied, reeling in her line. "Look at that. Nothing even touched my bait. Ready to head back?"

"Yeah, I'm kind of cold." Fran shivered.

They hung up their coats back at the cabin and Eu turned on the gas fireplace.

"Is there anything better than being inside with a fire when it's cold out?" Fran marveled.

"I know, I've been loving it," Eu agreed, sitting on the couch next to Fran and setting down two cups of hot tea with honey.

"I'm going to get spoiled being here." Fran grinned and picked up her tea cup.

"That's the goal," Eu said.

"Have you found out anything else about your mom since the last time we talked?"

"I found some things, but you stay here, and I'll go get them, because I'm hiding your Christmas presents in my room," Eu directed.

She'd been working on a painting for Fran that featured two pairs of sock-clad feet propped on her deck rail, with a view of the lake behind them. She'd bought the socks for inspiration and kept one pair while wrapping up the other pair to give to Fran. She'd also made a leather bracelet with her mother's kit.

She brought the painting supplies and leather kit, along with her mother's painting out to the dining room table, where Fran was waiting.

"Oh, this is so fun! We can go find some rocks and do that Zen thing where we paint them and leave them for people to find," Fran exclaimed, picking up the bottles of paint and examining the colors.

She put down a couple of different colors of blue and noticed the painting that Eu's mom had done of a little girl and her father, sobering immediately.

"Oh, my gosh, Eu. This is totally you and your dad," she breathed. "Just look at those shoulders."

Eu nodded. "Yeah, that's what I thought, too. I'm just trying not to read too much into things."

Studying the painting and lightly tracing over some of the lines with a fingertip, Fran's expression changed. "Look at how sad the little girl is. How sad you were," she murmured, raising her eyes to Eu, who glanced away.

Eu swallowed hard and picked up the leather making kit, setting it in front of Fran. "I thought this was really interesting."

Fran picked up one of the leather templates and studied it. "This looks familiar."

Eu nodded. “I thought so too, but I can’t for the life of me figure out why.”

Fran looked back at the painting, then at the template, then pointed to the painting, eyes wide. “Check it out – doesn’t this template look like the pattern on your dad’s belt in the painting?”

Eu felt the color drain from her face and her stomach clenched. “You’re right, that’s it! My dad did have a belt exactly like that. It’s been so long that I’d forgotten.”

“Do you think your mom might have made him that belt? Did they stay in touch?” Fran asked.

Eu shook her head. “Nope, no way, that’s impossible. My dad couldn’t even talk about her. He’d never answer any of my questions.” Inexplicably, her eyes filled with tears.

Fran set down the template and the painting. “You know what, I think we should go collect some perfectly Zen shaped rocks to paint.” She put her arm around Eu’s shoulders and gave them a squeeze. “We might be able to get a collection going before it’s time to get ready for the party.”

CHAPTER FIVE

"Holy moly!" Eu gasped when they pulled up to the gate in front of Benz Zoeller's mansion.

"Are you sure we're at the right address?" Fran asked. "I mean, no offense, but how in the world did you manage to get an invitation to this place?"

"Oddly, the guy who taught me how to clean catfish lives here," Eu replied, not pulling forward to the guard shack.

"Is he cute?" Fran giggled.

A horn honked behind them, startling them both, and Eu pulled forward, terrified that when she gave her name at the guard shack, she'd be turned away for some reason.

She held her breath when the guard checked his list and was relieved when he waved her through. A valet took her keys in front of the mansion and Eu and Fran walked slowly up the white marble steps, taking it all in.

"We don't belong here, Fran," Eu worried as they fell in line behind people who had been dropped off by limousines and luxury cars that she'd never heard of.

"You just stop that negativity. We have an invitation just like the rest of these people. Oh my gosh, I recognize that lady's dress! It was one of the originals from Next in Fashion. I can die happy now," Fran breathed, wide-eyed.

"We are out of our league," Eu whispered. "The bottle of wine that I brought is from the grocery store."

"I happen to like grocery store wine. Fake it till you make it, my friend," Fran replied, squaring her shoulders and lifting her chin a notch.

Eu did the same, trying to play it cool, but noticing the clothing and jewels that undoubtedly cost more than she'd ever made in her life, and excruciatingly aware of her spray-painted shoes and remade thrift shop outfit.

Relief only came when she saw Benz greeting guests at the door. He wore a tux and looked great, but his smile was the same one that he'd had when he taught her how to clean a catfish and somehow that made everything okay.

"Eugenia, you look great. Welcome," he said, hugging her lightly and kissing her cheek.

"Thanks, Benz, so do you. This is my friend Fran. She's visiting from L.A."

Benz saw Fran and seemed to freeze in place for a moment.

"Fran, it is indeed a pleasure," he said finally, giving her the same hug and kiss that he'd given Eu.

"Uh, likewise," Fran replied, admiration glowing in her eyes. "Thanks for letting me tag along with Eu."

"The pleasure is mine, truly."

A woman behind them cleared her throat delicately, snapping him out of his Fran-fueled trance.

"You ladies have a wonderful evening, and I'll catch up with you soon," he said, transitioning back into the perfect host.

"You didn't tell me he was gorgeous!" Fran hissed in Eu's ear as they walked away. "I think I'm in love."

"Looked pretty mutual from where I stood." Eu grinned. "Should we get a drink?"

"We should definitely get a drink," Fran replied, fanning herself.

"Coats please?" A uniformed young woman held out her hands, and they turned over their capes.

"If you have your invitation on your phone so I can get your names, I'll take your wine bottle over to the wine table and mark it for you," the coat check girl offered.

"I could get used to this," Fran remarked, after the coat girl whisked their capes and wine away.

"I don't think I could." Eu wrinkled her nose. "Way too much work. Let's get to the bar."

They each got a drink and decided to go exploring to see where everything at the party was located, and more importantly, what everyone was wearing.

They'd only ventured about ten feet from the bar when Fran froze, her mouth dropping open. "Oh, no!" she groaned.

"What?" Eu asked, baffled.

"The evil woman from the plane is here, no don't look over. Oh shoot, she just saw me and she's heading this way."

An older woman, with what looked like twenty pounds of garish makeup on her papery wrinkled face, strode over, martini in hand. She had overly large rings on every finger, and earrings that looked like they weighed a pound each.

"I don't know how you got an invite to this shindig, but I hope you don't spill someone's drink all over them." The woman smirked at Fran.

"Don't tempt me," Fran shot back, arching an eyebrow.

Before the woman could respond, another woman, who looked to be Eu's age, or maybe a bit younger, joined them.

"Oh, thank goodness, there are some non-dinosaurs at this party," she said, raising her glass to clink it against Eu's and Fran's. Close at her heels was an older man who smiled a little too brightly at them.

"I see you've met my grandma, Gabby…" the young woman began.

"Gabriella," the older woman corrected imperiously. Her granddaughter rolled her eyes.

"Gabriella," she said, in a comically affected way. "This is my grandpa, Bernie, uh Bernard, and I'm Clarissa."

"Nice to meet you, Clarissa. I'm Eugenia and this is Fran."

"Nice to meet you," Fran said, shooting a sideways glance at Gabby.

"You ladies look just lovely," Bernie said, giving them both the once-over.

"Thank you," the replied in unison.

"Go get me another drink, Bern," Gabby ordered, giving him a look.

"So, where are you from and what on earth are you doing in the Ozarks for Christmas?" Clarissa asked.

"My mom has a place up here," Eu said simply.

"We're from L.A," Fran chimed in. "What are you doing in the Ozarks?"

Clarissa leaned in as her grandmother guzzled the rest of her martini. "My grandparents won the lottery and bought a couple of franchises from Benz. I think he feels kind of obligated to invite them." She shrugged. "Personally, I come for the food and to people-watch. If you haven't tried the crab cakes yet, you should, they're the best."

Benz joined them then, wasting no time in asking Fran to dance. Before they hit the dance floor, he leaned in and told Eu to go to the bar and tell the bartender that she needed a modern Tom Collins. Then, with a wink, he swept Fran off to the dance floor.

Excusing herself and feeling more than a bit awkward, Eu went to the bar. When the heavily muscled bartender approached, she blushed. "I'm supposed to tell you that I need a modern Tom Collins, but I don't even know what that means," she confessed.

"What that means is that Benz was giving you a good way to get out of a conversation with someone." The bartender laughed. "I take it you were trapped by a boring guest?"

"Something like that." Eu laughed, relieved.

“Are you having a good time otherwise?”

“It’s a little overwhelming, to be honest. I feel really dumb because I didn’t know there would be a bar, so I brought a bottle of wine.”

“Oh, don’t worry about that at all. Lots of people who knew there’d be a bar brought a bottle of wine. They’re marked with the guests initials so that anyone who goes to the wine table can see what good taste they have.” He chuckled. “What can I get you to drink?”

“I’m driving tonight, so it’ll have to be a diet soda.”

“You’re one of the smart ones – that’s great. Just relax and have fun,” he said, handing her a glass of soda.

“I will – thanks.”

Eu turned from the bar, thinking that it might not be such a bad party after all, and across the room, she saw a woman glance at her, then stare at her, with a glare so profound that Eu swallowed hard and looked behind her to see if the woman was glaring at someone else.

When her gaze returned to the woman, Eu saw with dismay that she was headed her way with a stride that said she meant business.

"What are you doing here?" the woman, who looked oddly familiar, demanded, her tone dripping ice.

"I'm sorry. Have we met? You look very familiar," Eu replied, frowning.

"My sister gave birth to you." The woman made a face. "And I want to know what precisely is the reason that you are here?"

"You're my aunt?" Eu swayed slightly, feeling faint and wishing that she had more than diet soda in her glass. "That's why you look familiar."

"I'm nothing to you, and if you know what's good for you and remember your place, you'll leave here at your earliest opportunity, you money-grubbing nobody." The aunt gazed down at Eu's outfit, sneered, and stalked away, leaving behind the wreckage of what was almost a nice night out for Eu.

Finding the nearest pillar, Eu leaned against it, taking deep breaths and trying desperately to keep her knees from buckling beneath her.

Fran appeared out of nowhere, looking concerned. “Hey, are you okay? You’re really pale. I think you should sit down, and I’ll go get us some food,” she said, leading Eu over to a silk-clad sofa.

“I heard the crabcakes are good,” Eu mumbled, sipping at her drink.

Fran came back with two plates of food and ate with gusto, regaling Eu with tales of Benz’s wit and charm, while her friend picked at her plate, eating slowly.

Eu didn’t want to discuss what had happened while they were in public, so she smiled and nodded, encouraging Fran to keep chattering while she let the food nourish her darkened soul.

“Oh, wow, look outside,” Fran said suddenly, her mouth half full of stuffed mushroom.

“Why?” Eu said, her heart thumping.

“It’s starting to snow pretty heavily. As much as I’m loving this party, we should probably go soon. I’m guessing my L.A. bestie doesn’t know how to drive in the snow,” Fran replied.

"No, I don't, and I definitely don't want to risk Michael's car on bad roads," Eu agreed, relieved. "We should probably eat and run."

"Agreed," Fran nodded.

They finished eating and got their capes from the coat check girl, who also handed them gift bags to take with them. Benz hurried over when he saw them heading for the door.

"You ladies aren't thinking about going out in this mess, are you?" he asked.

"Yeah, we need to get home before it gets really bad out there," Fran replied.

"Lots of the guests are staying overnight you know. You two are more than welcome to stay – I have plenty of room," Benz offered.

"That's really sweet of you, but I feel like if we leave now, I can get us home safely," Eu said, hating the thought of potentially running into her aunt again.

"You're sure?" Benz looked concerned.

"Yep, we'll be fine. Thank you for inviting us," Fran said, giving him a bright smile.

"It was my pleasure, truly." He gave them both a hug and a kiss on the cheek, sending one of his valets to walk them to their car.

"You ladies be safe out there," the valet said, opening their doors.

They thanked him and began the white-knuckled drive home.

"Oh, man, I don't know if I'm more hungry or tired," Fran said with a giant yawn when they got back to the cabin.

"Same. How about we bring our pillows and comforters out to the couch and just snack and watch movies until we fall asleep?" Eu suggested.

"Slumber party, like the good old days. I love it." Fran grinned.

Eu forced a smile and headed down the hall to get into her pajamas. After what had turned out to be a painful party, which she'd share with Fran in the morning, she just didn't want to be alone.

CHAPTER SIX

As it turned out, falling asleep on the couch, next to her bestie, while watching a Christmas Hallmark movie, was exactly what Eu needed. She slept deeply, and when she woke up, Fran had coffee, bacon, and eggs ready.

"Morning, merry sunshine," Fran sang out, sliding perfectly cooked eggs onto plates. "Have you seen how deep the snow is out there? Holy moly! Do you want toast?"

"How much caffeine have you had this morning?" Eu asked, chuckling.

"Two cups so far, so you have some catching up to do." Fran pointed a spatula at her.

"I'll make the toast," Eu said as Fran placed their plates in front of the dining room chairs that had the best view of the lake. "Just set the butter on the table, please."

"You got it," Fran agreed.

"Somebody is awfully chipper this morning," Eu observed, bringing a plate of golden brown toast to the table.

"I can't help myself. I'm with you and there's all this beautiful snow…" Fran began.

"And you danced with a hot guy last night," Eu teased.

"Well, that might have a little something to do with it." Fran grinned and took a sip of coffee. "Now, when are you going to tell me about what happened to you last night? You were this weird shade of greyish green when I got to you. I thought I was going to have to carry you out of there," Fran said, sobering. "I was worried, Eu."

"I ran into someone…" Eu began, munching on a piece of bacon and reflecting upon how much better things looked after a good night's sleep.

"Not that horrific woman from the plane!" Fran blurted.

"No. My aunt. My mom's sister. And she was awful to me." Eu took a swig of coffee and told Fran what had transpired the night before.

"What a jerk! Why would she be so cruel?" Fran wondered.

Eu shook her head. "I have no idea, but it really freaked me out. I thought she looked familiar, and it was because she looked sort of like me."

"I'm sorry she was evil, but that says everything about her and nothing about you. She doesn't even know you and that's her loss." Fran reached over and hugged her friend.

"Yeah, I suppose so. Just struck me as strange that she seemed so bitter."

"Well, we're going to forget all about her today and have a wonderful day of doing absolutely nothing. Oh! But maybe we could go out later and build a snowman? I've never done that."

"Great idea," Eu agreed. "I haven't either."

“Then it’s settled. We’ll stay in our jammies until it’s snowman time,” Fran decreed.

“How do we do this?” Eu asked, standing on her dock, staring at the snow.

“I watched a YouTube video this morning, and I think we just make snowballs and roll them around until they’re big enough to make a snowman,” Fran replied. “Then we decorate it and go back inside where we belong.”

“Sounds like a plan, and we can put him close to the edge of the dock to make it look like he’s fishing,” Eu said, visualizing the finished project.

“Perfect! Let’s get a snowball started and make the bottom ball,” Fran replied, picking up two handfuls of snow and pressing them together.

She held the small ball while Eu packed more on so that they could get it big enough to roll. When it was about the size of a bowling ball, they rolled it up and down the dock until it was large enough.

"Whew, this is work," Fran commented, laughing. "I can't believe I'm winded from making a snowman."

"The altitude is higher here than what we're used to," Eu reminded her.

They made the second and third layers of the snowman, working together to lift them up onto the first large ball.

"Oh, my gosh, this is so cool," Fran exclaimed, her cheeks pink with cold and exertion.

"It kinda has to be so that he doesn't melt," Eu teased.

Fran rolled her eyes. "You just had to, didn't you?"

"Yep!" Eu laughed. "Now, let's get him finished. There's hot cocoa upstairs calling my name."

They found rocks for his eyes and mouth, and Eu had brought a carrot down to use for a nose. Fran tied a bit of fishing line with a bobber attached to it onto one of his stick arms to make it look like he was fishing, and they made a line of rocks down the front of the second tier to look like a shirt.

"I think he's mighty handsome," Eu said, as they stood back admiring their handiwork.

“I agree,” Fran said. “Now let’s get a selfie with him and stop talking about him before all these compliments go to his head. I’m ready for cocoa.”

“Me too,” Eu agreed, feeling more alive than she had in quite a while. They got on either side of their creation and took a selfie, then Eu grinned mischievously. “Race you to the door!” she challenged.

“Well, I don’t know,” Fran said slowly, then took off without warning.

“Hey, no fair!” Eu called out, laughing and trying to catch up with her friend.

Fran hit an icy patch in the snow and went down with a resounding whomp. Eu ran over to see if she was okay and landed with a thud right next to her. She heard Fran giggling and joined in, rolling toward her friend.

“You…should have…seen…how hilarious you looked,” Eu gasped, a fit of giggles holding her firmly in their grip.

“You should have seen the explosion of snow that went up when you landed,” Fran replied, laughing and wiping her eyes.

They sat up, still howling with laughter.

"Oh, man, my behind is getting wet from sitting in the snow," Fran said.

"Mine too. How in the world are we going to get up when we're surrounded by ice?" Eu asked, trying to get her giggles under control by taking deep breaths.

"I don't know, but you go first, because I've gotta see this."

"Rude," Eu said, as they both burst into laughter again. "Alrighty, here we go."

She tried to put her feet under her, but they kept sliding, so she rolled over onto her stomach, managed to get on her knees, and crawled over to the path that they'd taken on the way down to the dock. As soon as she got to her feet, she took off running.

"Hey, that's not fair!" she heard Fran call out, and a quick glance over her shoulder told her that her bestie was power crawling toward the path.

She arrived at her front door, out of breath, and watched with amusement as Fran slid to a stop on her heels seconds later.

"You cheated," Fran accused, giving Eu a playful nudge.

"You're the one who told me to go first. Fair is fair," Eu said. "Since I won, you can make the cocoa while I heat up some chocolate chip cookies."

"Deal," Fran agreed, as they stomped their running shoes to shed the snow before going inside.

When they took them off, their socks were caked in snow.

"Just throw them in the washing machine," Eu said, her cold fingers fumbling with the buttons on her coat.

Once they'd changed into warm, dry clothes, they sat in the living room, sipping cocoa and enjoying their cookies.

"It's a whole different world out here," Fran said with a smile, her cheeks still pink from the cold.

"Yeah, it almost doesn't feel like real life much of the time," Eu agreed.

Fran looked like she was about to reply when they suddenly heard a loud scraping from the parking lot.

"What on earth is that?" Fran asked, running to the foyer and opening the door. Eu was right behind her.

"Oh, wow, it's a snowplow," Eu remarked. "That's funny, we've had snow here before and there's never been a plow."

"Check it out, there's a couple of guys out there shoveling the sidewalks, too," Fran pointed, shivering.

"Interesting," Eu said. "First time for everything I guess."

"I think it's a sign," Fran said, closing the door and rubbing her upper arms.

"A sign? Of what?" Eu asked, as they headed back to the couch.

"That we should go to town and find a burger place for lunch. If this remote resort is plowed, you know the main roads have to be."

"That totally makes sense, and a burger that someone else makes for us sounds pretty amazing right now. Let's do it."

The besties had a leisurely lunch at a burger joint that had very little ambience, but fantastic food at great prices. They lingered for a while, eating the occasional French fry and sipping on their sodas, then paid their tab and wandered through the gift shop next door before heading back to the cabin. It was still bone-chilling cold out, but with full bellies and happy hearts they planned another day of relaxation.

They sat at the table painting rocks, and Eu had just finished the last spot on the wings of her ladybug rock when she looked out the window toward the dock.

"Hmm, that's weird," she mused. "I didn't think it was warm enough for our snowman to melt."

"That's just crazy talk," Fran replied, focused on the Zen circle that she was creating on her rock. "It's definitely not warm enough for him to melt. What makes you think he did?"

"Look. Doesn't it seem like he's misshapen or something?" Eu inclined her head toward the window.

Fran put down her paintbrush and looked. "Yeah, he definitely looks different. Let's go see what he's been up to. Maybe he caught a fish," she said lightly.

Eu couldn't dredge up a smile. Something about the snowman seemed off, and lately, whenever anything seemed off, bad news tended to be right around the corner.

They slipped into their coats and still wet shoes and headed out to the dock.

"That's weird," Fran said, as they approached the snowman. "He looks like he has something sticking out of his neck." She pointed, her mitten barely touching the snowman.

Eu brushed the snow away and gasped when she saw that there was a scarf wrapped around the snowman's neck…a hand painted silk scarf that she had planned to give Callie for Christmas.

"Eu, you're awfully pale, what's going on?" Fran asked.

"That scarf. I made it for Callie for Christmas. It was stashed in my closet," Eu murmured, still staring. "How on earth did it get out here?" She glanced back at the path that led to the dock, but since it had been neatly shoveled, there were no footprints between the dock and the house.

"Does anyone have your key?" Fran asked.

Eu shook her head, a sinking feeling making her stomach churn. "No. No one."

"Then you need to call the sheriff. I know they haven't always been the greatest, but you can't let something like this go. If someone broke into your house, they need to know."

"I really don't want to involve the police." Eu sighed, rushing over to get the scarf.

"But don't you think that this might be a message or something? We could be in danger here, Eu," Fran pointed out gently.

"Yeah, I suppose you're right. I just hate the thought of dealing with those deputies again. They'll probably try to figure out some way to blame it on me."

"I get it. But doing the right thing is rarely doing the easy thing," Fran replied, wrapping Eu in a hug. "But call from inside, it's freezing out here. I think my feet are about to fall off."

"Well, that would make it tough to surf," Eu said, managing a wan smile as she delicately peeled the scarf away from the snowman.

She called the sheriff's office to make a report once they were back inside and had put a pot of coffee on to brew, hoping that they'd send anyone other than her nemeses, Carter and Writman.

So of course, when she opened her door roughly an hour later, the grim faces of Carter and Writman filled her vision.

“Hi, come on in,” she said, trying not to sound too resigned. “I figured since I hadn’t seen you two in a few weeks, you might be missing me.”

“You were on our list to see today even before you called,” Writman replied.

CHAPTER SEVEN

"You've got to be kidding me. What could you possibly need from me?" Eu demanded with her hands on her hips as they stood in the foyer.

"Why don't we go to the living room and have a seat," Fran said, shooting Eu a reproachful look. "It's so cold out there. Can we offer you some coffee? Cocoa? Tea?"

"No, we're good, thanks," Carter replied, as the two deputies followed Fran to the living room.

Eu shut the door, shivering from the icy breeze that the deputies seemed to have brought in with them. She sat next to Fran on the sofa, while Carter sat perched on the edge of her leather recliner, and

Writman stood, staring down at them as though they'd just robbed a bank. He wasted no time with idle chit-chat. Eu doubted if he even knew how to engage in regular conversation.

"Why did you two leave Benz Zoeller's Christmas party early?" he asked.

Eu and Fran stared at him baffled for a moment, then Eu found her voice.

"Okay, first of all, how and why do you even know that? And secondly, we left the party early because we're from L.A. and I didn't want to have an accident on the way home because I don't know how to drive in snow."

"We know that you left early because we asked Mr. Zoeller if anyone had left the party. No one had but you. Everyone else stayed overnight," Carter explained.

Fran frowned. "Wait, I'm confused. Is it illegal to leave a party early?"

"It is if you killed someone before you did," Writman snapped, drawing a frustrated look from his partner.

"Say what?" Eu blurted. "Someone was killed at the party? Who?" she asked, aghast.

"Mrs. Gabriella Grange," Writman drawled. "Ring a bell?"

Eu shook her head. "No, not at all."

Fran's mouth dropped open. "Yes, it does ring a bell. That's the woman I sat next to on the plane."

"I understand there was a bit of an altercation on the plane," Carter said.

"Who told you that?" Eu bristled.

"Her husband. Is it true?" he asked Fran.

"Yes, it's true. I mean, it was silly, not a big deal or anything," Fran protested.

"And then another altercation at the party," Writman interrupted.

Eu couldn't keep silent. "Oh, please. That in no way could be considered an altercation. She was just being rude to Fran and Fran stood up for herself," she replied.

"I bet that made you angry, didn't it? Seeing her come at your friend like that." Writman smirked.

"Seriously? I think you've been watching too many crime shows," Eu replied, cocking an eyebrow at him.

Fran gave her a warning glance and spoke before Eu could really make Writman furious. "Look, neither disagreement was a big deal. I mean, I didn't particularly like the woman, but I certainly didn't kill her. And Eu isn't exactly the type to fly into a murderous rage either."

"She was drinking from a bottle of wine that you brought to the party," Writman said.

Eu frowned. "I'm shocked that anyone at that party drank it, but I wouldn't have been mad that she had some, even if we'd known."

Writman's eyes glittered as he pounced on her statement. "Why would you have been shocked that someone else drank your wine?" he asked, making it sound like an accusation.

Eu gave him a withering glance. "Because it's cheap. I bought it at the grocery store and the people at that event aren't grocery store wine people."

"Then why did you bring it?" His expression was skeptical, and he folded his arms.

"Because even poor people know not to show up to a party empty handed," Eu replied, glaring.

Writman glanced around the cabin's lovely interior. "Poor people? Don't look like you're hurting too bad."

"So why did you call us out here?" Carter interjected, in what looked like an attempt to bring down the emotional temperature in the room.

"Well, it seems pretty lame now, all things considered, but somehow, while we were in town having a burger, someone had to have gotten inside the house. They took a scarf and put it on the snowman we built yesterday," Eu replied.

The deputies exchanged a look, so quickly that Eu found herself wondering if she'd imagined it.

"Do you have the scarf?" Carter asked.

"Yes, it's in the dryer," Eu replied.

"Why is it in the dryer?" Writman asked, eyes narrowed.

Eu frowned. "Because it had snow on it."

"Can we see it?" Carter asked.

"Yeah, hang on. I'll go get it," Eu replied, heading down the hall to the laundry area. She came back holding the scarf.

"Whose is it?" Carter asked, snapping on a nitrile glove and taking it from her by touching one small corner.

"Technically, it's mine. I bought a silk painting kit and made it as a gift."

"For who?" Writman asked.

"For whom," Eu corrected. "And it was for Callie. She lives across the parking lot. You've met her before."

"Yeah, I remember. And I'm supposed to believe that you two are besties now?" Writman challenged.

"No, not at all, but I'm certainly not going to give up on making friends with her when we're the only people in the resort all winter," Eu shot back.

"Gabriella's granddaughter was attacked by a would-be strangler who used something that felt like a silk scarf, after her grandmother passed. I'm going to need to collect the lint from your dryer," Carter said.

"It's down the hall and to the right, behind the folding doors. Oh, my gosh, poor Clarissa, is she okay?" Eu called after Carter, who didn't respond.

Writman stared at her.

"Sounds like someone has it out for that family," Fran said. "How awful."

"Yeah, awful," Writman replied, gazing at both of them in turn.

"Where's the snowman?" Carter asked, tucking an evidence bag full of lint into his pocket.

"On my dock," Eu pointed.

He and Writman moved toward the door and left the house.

"Thanks for cleaning my dryer trap," Eu called after them.

"Seriously?" Fran muttered, elbowing her. "I can't believe she's dead." She shook her head.

"Yeah, and you'd better believe they're going to try to blame you for it," Eu replied.

CHAPTER EIGHT

After a quiet dinner, where neither Fran nor Eu ate very much, the two of them sat on the couch looking through internet articles on their phones, trying to find information about the Grange case.

"Oh, no," Fran muttered.

"What?" Eu's stomach dropped.

"Gabby was poisoned. I bet that's why they brought up that she'd been drinking the wine that we brought. They think we poisoned her. They think I poisoned her," Fran whispered.

Eu shook her head, the idea too terrible to even think about. "Nope, no way. You flew in from L.A, it's not like you brought poison with you in your suitcase, that's ridiculous."

"Yeah, ridiculous for me to bring it with me, but you live here. I could have taken something from under your sink to use." Fran paled.

Eu sighed. "Well, here we go again. I'd really like to get through at least one season without being suspected of doing something that I didn't do."

"I'm so sorry, Eu. If I hadn't been nasty on the plane and at the party, we wouldn't be in this mess. So now what do we do?"

"Don't worry, it's not your fault. We're outsiders. We'll just do the same thing I've done in the past. Deputy Dawg and his hostile sidekick sourpuss aren't going to solve this thing, so we're going to have to."

Fran gave her a lopsided grin. "While I hate that you've had to become this Nancy Drew person since you've been here, it's also kind of awesome," she said, looking at her bestie with admiration.

"It'll be awesome when it's over and hopefully I can start figuring out more about my mom so that I can leave here in the spring, if not before," Eu replied.

"I thought you liked it out here," Fran said, tilting her head to the side.

Eu nodded. "I do. But I don't know if I'll ever be accepted."

"Oh, who cares what those cops think? Everyone else out here seems really nice. Especially that Benz," Fran said, affecting a dreamy-eyed gaze and batting her eyes.

Eu chuckled. "What is it with us and older guys these days?" she asked, shaking her head.

Fran laughed. "No idea. I have a good dad, and you *had* a good dad, so clearly that's not it."

"Maybe we're both just too mature for guys our age," Eu mused.

"Well, I don't know about you, but this mature girl is going to get into her fuzzy jammies and have cocoa and a snack."

Eu smiled. "I'm so with you on that. Board games?"

"You're on. And you're going down," Fran warned.

After yet another mellow evening where they played games and watched television until they were both yawning, Eu tossed and turned in her bed, thinking about how someone had been in her house. Shivering with cold and worry, she got out of bed and moved quietly down the hall, to double lock the slider in the living room and place the back of a dining room chair under the front doorknob. Just as she'd placed the chair under the knob, Fran, who had apparently snuck down the hall, yelled freeze, and flipped on the light.

Eu screamed. Fran screamed. And when they both saw each other, they wilted with relief.

"Oh, my gosh, I thought you were a burglar when I heard sounds," Fran gasped.

"Sorry about that. I just couldn't sleep after everything that happened, so I figured that I might as well come out here and make sure that the cabin was as safe as I could make it," Eu admitted.

"I think now that I know things have been reinforced, I might actually get some sleep," Fran said, hugging her bestie. "How about you?"

"Yeah, I think so," Eu replied, stifling a yawn.

They both padded back down the hall to their rooms and slept soundly until a knock sounded on the front door the next morning, startling them both awake.

"Seriously? The police are coming around this early?" Eu grumbled, tossing a robe on over her pajamas and yawning hugely. Fran came out of her room and trailed behind her.

Eu put the dining room chair back and opened the door, a grumpy frown on her face. Much to her surprise, it was Clarissa standing on her porch, not the deputies.

"Oh, uh, I'm sorry. Did I wake you?" she asked, glancing down at her phone to check the time.

Eu stared at her for a moment trying to get her wits about her. "No worries, what time is it?" she asked, covering a yawn with her hand.

"It's like 9:30. Are you okay?" Clarissa peered at her, looking concerned.

"Yeah, we're all good. We were up late," Eu said with a smile.

"I'm sorry to just show up like this. I just, I don't really know what to do with myself while I'm staying here waiting for news about my grandma."

"No apologies, really. It's all good. Do you want to come in for some coffee?"

Clarissa nodded. “Yeah, coffee would be great. The new cook my grandpa got makes horrible coffee.”

“We’re so sorry about your grandma,” Fran said. Eu nodded.

“Thanks. It’s been pretty rough. Hard to sleep. Hard to eat.” Clarissa sighed. “I got your address from Benz because I desperately needed some girl time.”

“Well, you came to the right place,” Eu assured her. “I’ll heat up some of the best cinnamon rolls that you’ll ever put in your mouth, and you can wash it down with nice fresh coffee that will hopefully be better than your cook’s.”

“That’s not a really high bar to clear,” Clarissa said, with a half-smile.

They settled in with coffee and Michael’s cinnamon rolls and Eu was pleased to see that Clarissa was picking off little bites and eating them.

“So, have the police made any progress on the investigation?” Fran asked.

Clarissa shrugged. “I don’t really know. They’re not really keeping in touch with me and my grandpa is just a basket case. They said it could’ve been anyone.

She rubbed a lot of people the wrong way, but that's only because it was hard to get to know her. She had a good heart," she said sadly.

"So, was there anyone who stood out to you that you think might have done it?" Eu asked.

"Not that I can think of, although there was this one awful woman who was flirting with my grandpa all night, now that I think of it," Clarissa mused.

"What did she look like?" Fran asked.

"She had this very Cruella de Vil look about her. Sharp features. Black dress with white trim. Nails filed to points and painted red. Like blood red. Platinum hair."

Eu swallowed hard and nodded, unable to speak. She knew who Clarissa was talking about. She'd very accurately described Eu's aunt, and Eu was not looking forward to the conversation that she would now have to have with that particularly unpleasant woman.

"I love your cabin. It's cozy. Have you lived here long?" Clarissa changed the subject.

"Uh, no. I came here from L.A. a couple months ago."

"Why in the world would you want to come here from L.A?"

"I'm just interested in finding out more about my mom," Eu replied.

"What do you do for a living, Clarissa?" Fran changed the subject, likely because she knew that Eu would be uncomfortable sharing more about her situation with a stranger, even a nice one like Clarissa.

"I'm working on getting my photography business up and running, actually. I take care of my grandparent's house when they travel, since I have an apartment in their basement. My mom and dad died in a car crash when I was little. My grandpa raised me with my real grandma until she passed a few years ago. Gabby was his second wife. These cinnamon rolls are really good. It's nice to almost feel hungry again." She smiled faintly.

"I wish I could take credit for them, but I didn't make them. A guy who has a cabin in the complex likes to bake," Eu confided.

"Nice! Is he single?" Clarissa grinned.

"I have no idea. I never asked, but he's older than I am," Eu said, blushing.

"Nothing wrong with a sugar daddy, especially one who bakes." Clarissa chuckled. "So, what's there to do around here?"

"Well, I've been enjoying fishing, and I've heard there are some beautiful hiking trails around here too," Eu said.

Clarissa shuddered. "I'm not exactly the outdoorsy type. I'm only here because they made me come. I think they wanted someone to carry their luggage. I didn't even get to sit in first class with them. I was back in coach, making the most out of my tiny bag of pretzels." She let out a humorless laugh.

"Well, it's nice to be needed," Fran said.

They all laughed.

"I should probably get going. Seriously though, thanks so much for the company and the goodies. It was just what I needed," Clarissa said.

Eu wrapped up a cinnamon roll and handed it to her.

"Thanks for dropping by. It was good seeing you again, even if not under the best of circumstances," she said, walking her to the door.

"Same. If you two get bored and want to come do something that's not nature related, you should come see me. We're at the Farnsworth Resort. Just give them my name at the gate and they'll let you in. We're in Unit 2. You can't miss it. Every ostentatious place in there has the house number prominently displayed out front."

"Thanks for the invitation, we may just do that," Eu said, laughing.

Clarissa shut the door behind herself, and Eu and Fran went back to the kitchen for more coffee.

"Wasn't that your aunt that she was talking about as a possible suspect?" Fran asked in a low voice.

"It was indeed. But what Clarissa didn't see that I did see, was that her grandfather wasn't just flirting with my aunt. He flirted with any woman who came within six feet of him."

Fran nodded. "Come to think of it, he was that way on the plane, too. It was annoying and I think he even was a bit much."

"We're going to have to talk to both my aunt and the grandpa now," Eu said, thinking. "We can get to him by going over to visit Clarissa, but I have no idea how to get to my aunt."

"I'll text Benz, he'll know," Fran replied, pulling her phone out of the pocket of her pajama pants.

"You're texting each other now? That escalated quickly," Eu teased.

Fran blushed. "Oh, stop. He just wanted to make sure that I had his number in case we needed anything."

"Uh huh, even though I already have it?" Eu gave her a look.

"Hey, you have the hot professor. Let me have some fun," Fran replied. "So, who do we talk to first, Nancy Drew?"

Eu thought for a moment. "Well, I'd like to believe that I don't have homicidal people in my own family line, so let's talk to dear old grandpa first."

"Sounds like a plan," Fran agreed. "We'll have to wear something pretty." She gave Eu a wicked grin.

CHAPTER NINE

"Wow, this looks sort of like Benz's neighborhood except that the houses don't have as much land around them," Fran said, as they pulled up to Farnsworth Resort, the gated community where Clarissa's grandparents owned a vacation home.

"Now let's just hope they let us in," Eu replied, pulling up to the guard shack.

They gave the guard Clarissa's name, and he waved them through. The massive homes were decorated with Christmas lights that sparkled beneath the snow. It looked like fairyland. A very expensive fairyland.

They found Unit 2 and pulled into the circular drive.

"I hope it's okay to leave the car here," Eu said, looking for parking spaces.

"I'm sure it's fine. Now, as long as we don't slip on all that white marble between us and the door, we'll be all set." Fran chuckled.

A uniformed maid answered the door, gave them each a pair of slippers wrapped in plastic so that they could leave their shoes on a drying rack by the door, and showed them into a living room that could've belonged to Louis the 15th.

"Someone has way too much affection for the Victorian Era," Fran mused, taking in the décor.

"Shhh. They may have security cameras in here," Eu whispered, feeling supremely uncomfortable wearing slippers that weren't hers.

"Doubtful. This is all reproduction stuff. I doubt there's an authentic piece in the room," Fran replied, plopping down onto a sculpted velvet settee.

"Hey, you guys decided to come over!" Clarissa came into the room, looking surprised. "Thank goodness, I've been bored out of my mind. What do you want to do? Watch a movie, play video games, raid the liquor cabinet and get wasted?" She chuckled.

"We're good with just hanging out and doing whatever," Eu replied.

"Cool, let's go to the rec room then. This place is way too stuffy for my taste." Clarissa glanced around the room and rolled her eyes.

They climbed a red carpeted marble staircase and went through a maze of dark wood-paneled hallways before entering a room that looked as though it had been decorated by George Jetson. It had arcade games, ping-pong, a pool table, a lounge with a fully stocked bar, and a private theater.

"This is amazing. I don't think I'd ever leave this room," Eu said.

"Yeah, it's the only room in the house that doesn't look like you just stepped back in time. Are you guys hungry? Would you like some snacks?" Clarissa asked.

Fran's stomach growled audibly, and they all laughed.

"Well, that answers that," Clarissa said, pressing a button on the bar.

An accented woman's voice came through a speaker and Clarissa ordered snacks. Eu thought it was strange that she didn't specify what types of snacks but figured that maybe the maid knew her well enough to know her preferences.

"You're living the good life, girl," Fran commented, sinking into a leather sofa. "Were your grandparents always wealthy? Even before they won the lottery?"

Clarissa snorted. "Heck no. I was raised in a trailer, and it wasn't even a nice trailer."

Eu nodded. "I come from pretty humble beginnings, too."

Fran leaned forward, peering at Clarissa. "I feel like I know you from somewhere. Have you ever been to L.A?"

Clarissa laughed. "Aside from the couple of times that my grandpa got courtside tickets to a Lakers game, no."

Eu studied Clarissa's face too. "Yeah, you do seem familiar," she agreed.

"Guess I just have one of those faces."

They chatted for a few minutes, until they heard a discreet knock on the rec room door, followed by another uniformed maid entering with a cart full of food, which she took to one of the tables in the room, setting out pizzas, hotdogs, nachos, and a host of other delicious choices.

"I could live here for a month and never eat all that food," Fran said, grabbing one of the China plates that the maid set out.

"Challenge accepted," Clarissa said with a grin.

Eu wondered how she stayed so rail-thin while surrounded by every snack food known to mankind.

"Well, hello there, ladies!" Bernie, Clarissa's grandpa, greeted them, appearing in the doorway. "I saw Maria fixing up a feast and figured I'd come say hello. Say, didn't I meet you two gals the other night?" he asked, helping himself to a deviled egg.

"Yes, that was us," Fran replied, batting her eyes a bit. "I'm surprised you remembered – there were so many people there."

"I never forget lovely ladies," Bernie said with a wink. "Did Rissy give you a tour of the house?"

"No, not yet," Fran said. "But we'd love to see it."

"Well then, you just come see me after you're done with your snack, and I'll be happy to show you around."

"Sounds great," Eu said. Fran nodded.

Bernie snagged another deviled egg and waved on his way out.

"He thinks this place is the Taj Mahal," Clarissa joked, after Bernie and the maid had gone.

"Well, it's understandable that he'd be proud since he came from less fortunate circumstances," Eu replied. "I'm glad he's keeping his spirits up after what happened."

"Yeah, he has good times and bad times." Clarissa shrugged, taking a bite of pepperoni pizza.

"We heard that you were attacked, too," Fran said gently. "That must've been so scary. Do the police have any leads yet?"

Clarissa's eyes flooded with tears, and she shook her head. After a moment, she took a sip of sparkling water and swallowed hard. "I'm trying not to think about it right now," she said, finally.

"Totally understandable. So, what movies do you have in here?" Eu asked, shooting Fran a look.

They all took more food and started on an animated discussion of their favorite movies and the awkward moment passed. They were laughing about a particular rom com that they'd all seen when Clarissa's phone rang.

She looked at it and frowned. "I'm sorry, I have to take this. If you really want a tour of the house, just hit the button on the bar and Maria will take you to my grandpa." She gave them an apologetic look and hurried from the room.

Eu and Fran exchanged a look.

"Well, that was easy," Fran whispered.

"Right?" Eu said. "We'll have time alone to talk to the person who was closest to the victim."

"And in the movies, it's always the husband. He seemed kind of too happy for a grieving spouse, don't you think?" Fran said.

"I guess we'll find out," Eu said, pushing the button to call the maid.

CHAPTER TEN

Maria led them through the paneled hallways until they were nearly back to the stairs and stopped in front of a thick mahogany door. She knocked softly on it, then opened it.

Bernie was sitting at an oversized desk, looking intently at his phone, but he glanced up and brightened when he saw Eu and Fran. "Well, hello again, ladies! Welcome to my study." He stood and raised his arms, turning in a circle.

Eu felt supremely uncomfortable in the room that had a seemingly endless supply of animals and fish that had obviously been subjected to the work of a skilled taxidermist. Beneath the woodland displays were several heavy wooden gun cabinets and lighted shelves with knives of all shapes and sizes on them.

“That’s quite an arsenal you have there,” Fran remarked.

“You betcha. I wasn’t always an old codger. I was a strong young buck once upon a time and I had to hunt so that we could eat.”

“You must’ve been a pretty good shot.” Fran flirted.

Bernie’s chest puffed up. “I could hold my own, young lady.” He grinned. “Now, let me show you the old homestead.”

He took them through a grand library, a sunroom that looked like it had never been used, and countless other rooms that were all decorated to the hilt.

“You have a beautiful home,” Eu said, though it was far too ostentatious for her taste.

“Coming from such a beautiful lady, I’ll take that as a compliment,” Bernie replied with a wink.

“So, how are you holding up, Bernard?” Fran asked.

He stared at her blankly. “Uh, call me Bernie,” he said, finally.

"We're so sorry for your loss, Bernie," Eu prompted.

He nodded, his eyes taking on a faraway look. "Oh, yes. Terrible thing. Don't know who would do such a thing." He was quiet for a moment, then spoke again. "Oh, I remember, I haven't shown you the spa room. Let's head down there."

Fran and Eu exchange a look. After showing them a lower level of the house that any Beverly Hills clinic would envy, he stopped and thought for a moment.

"Ladies, I'm sorry. I just remembered something that I need to take care of." He tapped on his phone and the maid answered. "Maria, would you come down to the spa and take Rissy's guests back to the recreation room?"

"Enjoy your visit and ask Rissy to show you the miniature golf course. I think you might like it. I became a great putter on that course," Bernie said, his smile not quite reaching his eyes.

The maid appeared and led them back to the rec room, where Clarissa was nowhere to be found. Fran picked up a piece of pizza and took a bite, chewing thoughtfully.

"Interesting," Eu said, her appetite gone.

Fran looked at her intently, then flicked her eyes upward, toward the corner of the room. Sure enough, there was a security camera there. Eu nodded and spoke again.

"I've never seen a spa quite as luxurious as that one. Clarissa is so lucky to live in this amazing house."

"I know right?" Fran replied, her mouth half full. "I wonder where she is?"

They both sounded a bit like they were reading from a script, but each knew that they had to play it off like they didn't know that they might have someone watching and listening.

"Yeah, I hope everything is okay. You know, since she's taking kind of a long time, she may not feel like company when she's done. Maybe we should go and come back another time," Fran suggested, popping the last bite of pizza in her mouth.

"Yeah, you're probably right. We can check on her later and make sure she's okay. It's gotta be hard having something so awful happen to your grandma," Eu agreed. "I'll leave her a note to let her know we had to go."

The friends moved at a reasonably slow pace, fully aware that they might be in the house with a man who killed his wife, and not wanting to tip him off. Once Eu finished the note for Clarissa, she pushed the button to ring for the maid, feeling guilty about summoning someone in that manner.

She led them back to the front door and insisted that they keep their slippers. They thanked her and left, neither of them relaxing until they got into the car.

"Okay, so, here's what we know..." Eu began. "Grandpa doesn't look terribly sad, he has a roomful of deadly weapons, and when we mentioned his wife, he couldn't get rid of us fast enough."

Fran nodded. "All true, but we need to do our due diligence and talk to your aunt as well."

Eu sighed. "Yeah, I agree, but I need another day to prepare myself for that encounter," she admitted.

"Understandable. So, painting rocks and watching Christmas movies tonight?" Fran suggested with a grin.

"Definitely. And maybe some baked goods thrown in there." Eu smiled.

"Uh yeah, that goes without saying," Fran replied, laughing.

Eu froze when she pulled into the parking space. "Oh, no, Fran look."

The door to the cabin was wide open.

"Did you forget to close it or lock it?" Fran whispered, her eyes wide.

"No. I totally remember making sure it was tightly closed, and I turned the key before we left," Eu replied.

"Oh, man, I don't want to go in there." Fran sighed, gripping the dashboard.

"I don't either, but we have to," Eu said. "It could be just a coincidence."

"Uh-huh," Fran replied, not sounding at all convinced.

They got out, shutting the car doors as quietly as they could, and moved slowly toward the porch.

Eu's heart thumped in her throat and her hands shook, but she stepped across the threshold anyway. At first it seemed like nothing was amiss, but when they peered in the door of Eu's bedroom, the covers of her bed were flung back, with the pillows askew. Eu gasped.

"What?" Fran whispered.

"I made the bed this morning. I'm one hundred percent positive," Eu replied.

"Of course you did, you always do. I did too, so let's go check the guest room," Fran suggested.

They crossed the hall and saw that Fran's bed was the same way.

"You check all of your things and make sure that nothing has been stolen, and I'll do the same," Eu said. "And let's get these windows closed. Why would someone open every window?"

"I have no idea, but this is weird."

Eu nodded. "Normally, I'd say that we need to call the police, but…"

"There's no point," Fran finished her sentence. "I just don't understand how someone could've opened the door. There weren't any weird marks on it like someone broke in."

"Yeah, it makes me wish that the resort hadn't plowed, so that we could see footprints," Eu replied. "I just can't imagine who would do this, though." She frowned.

Fran's mouth fell open. "Wait! Did your aunt send you the keys for this place?" she asked, clutching at Eu's arm.

"Yeah, why?"

"Because she could have kept a copy and she's in town. Maybe she's trying to send you a message?" Fran proposed.

Eu nodded. "Maybe so. If that's the case, I don't care if she's a stone-cold killer, she's going to get a piece of my mind."

CHAPTER ELEVEN

"Okay, we've had our breakfast, and I've gotten your aunt's address from Benz, so we need to dress nicely, do our hair and makeup and go face the dragon," Fran said, after downing the last drops of her coffee.

"Yeah, I know. I have a feeling that this conversation isn't going to be nearly as pleasant as the one with Bernie was, whether she's the killer or not." Eu sighed.

"Are you sure you want me to go with you for this one?" Fran asked. "I mean, in a weird, dysfunctional kind of way, she's family, so if you want to be alone with her, I totally get that."

Eu raised her chin and looked Fran in the eye. "You're more of a family to me than she'll ever be. Of course I want you there."

Fran reached across the table and squeezed Eu's hand. "Alright then, girl, let's do this."

They both went to their rooms to get ready and regrouped in the living room roughly half an hour later.

"You look fabulous," Fran proclaimed. "To the batmobile."

Despite her nervousness, Eu laughed at her friend's antics and headed for the door.

Her mouth went dry as they pulled up to the gates of an estate that was far grander than Benz's in every way. Clarissa's grandparents' home looked like an apartment by comparison.

"Well, we're definitely getting the tour of lifestyles of the rich and shameless this week, aren't we?" Fran commented dryly.

"I don't know if I can do this," Eu said, her stomach churning.

"You can absolutely do this. I've got your back. Nothing she says can hurt you because she doesn't know you at all," Fran said gently.

"Alright. Let's go before I chicken out." Eu sighed and opened her door.

The doorbell played a classical tune, and a very pleasant maid answered the door.

"Hello, we're here to see Mauricia Bellingham, please," Eu said.

"Please come in," the maid invited.

She showed them to a stylishly modern sitting room and soon after, an elegant woman entered the room, seeming astonished when she saw Eu.

"You must be Eugenia," she said breathlessly, holding out her hand. "Forgive me. You look so much like your mother that I was certain I'd seen a ghost. I'm Brigitte Wellsley. Your auntie Mauricia is staying with me for the holidays. Welcome. Can I bring you anything?"

"No, we're fine, thanks," Eu replied.

"Well then, I'll send Mauricia in and you can chat. Such a pleasure meeting you." Brigitte smiled fondly at Eu, then left, shutting the double doors to the sitting room behind her.

“I hope your aunt is as nice as Brigitte is,” Fran whispered.

“She’s not,” Eu said dryly, making a face.

The doors burst open just then, and a pale, dark-haired woman entered and gave them a disapproving look.

“I have no idea why you would’ve had the audacity to come here uninvited,” Mauricia said, her words like ice.

Eu swallowed, trying hard to keep the myriad of emotions warring within her in check. “Is it so bad that I want to get to know my aunt a little bit?” she asked.

“You have nothing to gain from coming to me. I would’ve thought you’d be grateful for what my misguided sister gave you, not that you’d be sniffing around begging for more.” Mauricia arched an eyebrow.

“How dare you…” Eu began. Fran put a hand on her arm.

"Look, why don't we just take things down a notch and start over," Fran suggested.

Eu shook Fran's hand off and strode to her aunt, her chin jutting out defiantly. "You don't even know me. The reason I came here has nothing to do with begging. I came here to ask you for the spare key to my cabin. There's no reason that you should have it."

"I have no idea what you're talking about. Why would I have a key to whatever rustic little treehouse my sister had? I sent everything to you because I wanted nothing to do with the disposal of her oddities." Mauricia seemed entirely unmoved by Eu's emotional response, merely staring at her with disdain.

"Wow, are you hearing yourself right now? Your sister passed and you talk about her as though she was nothing more than gum on the sole of your ridiculous designer shoe," Eu said, her teeth gritted so hard that her teeth ground against each other.

A muscle in aunt's jaw rippled as her jaws clenched.

"Don't you dare talk to me about my sister. You of all people have no right to talk to me about her." Mauricia looked for a moment like the cool façade she'd maintained might finally crack, but she took a breath, and the dead look of a predatory shark returned to her eyes. "You can show yourself out, and don't darken my doorstep again."

"Actually, I believe this is Brigitte's doorstep," Fran called after her as she slammed the doors shut behind herself.

"That went well," Eu said. "If my mother was like that, I don't think I want to know."

Fran nudged her and put an arm over her shoulders as they headed to the doors. "Hey, she produced you. She can't have been that bad. I'd be willing to bet if that awful Mauricia had kids, they'd pull the legs off of spiders and feed live mice to snakes."

Eu smiled faintly, appreciating that Fran was trying to lighten the mood. "And they'd howl by the light of the full moon."

CHAPTER TWELVE

"So, we're obviously looking for someone who can pick locks," Fran said, after they checked the house for evidence of an intruder. There was none.

"Apparently, although I wouldn't put it past my mother's sister to lie. I wonder what she would have been looking for though, and why she messed up the beds," Eu mused.

"I think she messed up the beds so that we'd be freaked out, but she may have been looking for whatever might be in your mother's hidden places."

"Some old photos, a hair ribbon and some art supplies? Why would she want that?" Eu wondered aloud. "That doesn't make sense."

"Is that everything that you've found?" Fran asked.

Eu thought for a moment, then inspiration struck. "No, it isn't! When I was vacuuming after I first got here, I vacuumed under the bed and heard this clanking sound on the roller. When I got down on the carpet and looked, I found a little key."

"Like a house key?" Fran asked.

"No, it was smaller. Like a jewelry box key or something. Hang on, I'll go get it." Eu dashed back to her room and took it from where she'd hidden it in between the pages of a novel.

"This is it," she said, handing it over.

"Hmm…I wonder what the letters and numbers mean. NBO 017," Fran murmured. "It's too short to be a phone number. I wonder if it's some kind of code. Did you google it?"

Eu stared at her. "You know, I can't believe this, but I never even thought of that. Let's see if we can figure out what the numbers might mean."

"You google the numbers and letters, and I'll do a photo search with my phone," Fran said, snapping a picture of the key and searching for matches online.

"I'm not coming up with anything," Eu said a few minutes later.

"Yeah. The only thing I've discovered is that it's probably brass and is fairly old. I'm not even getting any results for what kind of key it is," Fran replied.

Eu sighed. "Well, we tried. I wonder if this is what she was after," she said, turning the key over in her palm.

"And I wonder if there are any other surprises under the beds," Fran said in a moment of inspiration.

"I checked under mine when I found the key, but I didn't check under yours," Eu replied.

They scrambled up and headed for the guest room, dropping to their stomachs to search under the bed. Unfortunately, no more clues turned up.

"You know, I've heard that people sometimes hide things below drawers, maybe we should check the furniture and built ins in the closet and kitchen," Fran suggested.

"Nah, that's too obvious, but what if she attached something to the back of the drawer? No one ever sees the back of a drawer unless they're demolishing it," Eu replied.

"I can't believe it. Nothing, zip, zilch, nada," Eu said, as she and Fran flopped down onto the couch, feeling overly warm and slightly dusty.

"Well, as least every drawer in the house got a nice cleaning." Fran laughed.

"Oh, my gosh, we went full on Scooby Doo, didn't we?" Eu giggled.

"Yeah, but I'm pretty sure Shaggy and the gang would have figured out what the mystery key goes to, or what the code means by now," Fran said.

"Where's Shaggy when you need him?" Eu sighed dramatically, flinging an arm across her eyes.

There was a loud knock on the door.

"That must be him," Fran said, sending them into a fit of giggles.

Eu was still laughing when she opened the door but sobered immediately when she looked into the grim faces of Carter and Writman.

"Daily drive-by?" Eu asked. She heard Fran snort behind her and had to bite the inside of her cheek to keep from bursting into laughter.

"Which one of you has a light blue ski jacket?" Writman asked, clearly not amused.

"That's me, why?" Fran stepped around Eu and stared at the deputies.

"We'd like to take a look at it," Carter replied. "Please."

"Got a warrant?" Eu blurted, before Fran could answer.

"You really want to play that game again?" Writman's tone was thunderous. Clearly a storm was brewing in the man.

"No games at all. I have nothing to hide," Fran said defiantly.

"No, but you do have rights," Eu said, shooting her a direct look.

"I'm aware. I've dealt with L.A. cops, I'm sure these two are harmless, aren't you fellas?" Fran said, giving them a flirty smile.

Eu gritted her teeth. "Like a bear in the woods is harmless," she said dryly.

"Where is the coat?" Carter asked.

Fran dragged Eu out of the way and said, "follow me." She opened the foyer coat closet with a flourish and pointed out her coat, which looked bright and fun next to the practical black puffer coat that Eu had found at the thrift store.

Carter snapped on a pair of nitrile gloves and grabbed the coat, immediately digging his hand into the right pocket. "Found it," he said, pulling out a silver pen and a small glass vial.

"I've never seen either of those things before," Fran said, the color draining from her face as Eu gave her an exasperated look.

"Yeah, we hear that a lot," Writman said, holding out an evidence baggie. Carter dropped the pen and vial into it and took off his gloves.

“Wait a minute,” Eu said. “How did you know what color her coat was and how to magically find two items in her pocket that she didn’t even know were there?”

“There was a witness,” Carter replied.

CHAPTER THIRTEEN

"What are you talking about? A witness to what?" Fran demanded. "I told you, I've never seen those items and I have no idea how they got in my pocket."

"Mr. Grange called us to report that a pen was missing from his desk after he gave you two a tour of his house today," Carter explained.

"Well then maybe you should look into Mr. Grange, instead of Fran," Eu said, furious. "Clearly he set us up. We went over to visit Clarissa, and he insisted upon giving us a tour of his house. Obviously he did it so that he could frame us."

"That man just lost his wife," Writman growled. "Y'all best be watching your p's and q's, young lady."

"Don't you threaten me. That man who just lost his wife was flirting with every woman in the room and tried to get flirty with us today, too. Did you ever stop to think that she was awful to live with and he was trying to get rid of her and blame it on someone else?" Eu challenged.

"Nice try. He reported his pen missing, the maid said she saw you slip something into your pocket, and what do you know, here it is in your pocket. It doesn't take a rocket scientist to figure that one out," Writman drawled.

"Wow, Maria helped set us up?" Fran said sadly. "She seemed so nice."

"And what about that little bottle thingie, whatever it is." Eu gestured toward the evidence bag.

"My guess is that there's gonna be residue inside it that matches the poison that killed Mrs. Grange. And if so, you're in a whole heap of trouble, ma'am," Writman warned Fran, then turned to Eu. "And you'll be looking at aiding and abetting a felony. That's definitely worthy of some quality time in a federal facility."

"There's a storm coming," Carter interrupted his partner. "We're not taking you into custody because we're full up and it ain't like you're gonna leave town in a blizzard. Just sit tight while we investigate, and we'll get back with you."

"Custody?" Fran's eyes widened. "You've got to be kidding me. I've never even been to traffic court. I've never had a parking ticket," she said, dazed.

Eu stared directly at Carter, knowing that Writman was a lost cause. "You know this is all too convenient. Eyewitness tips leading to you finding," she made air quotes, "evidence of a petty crime and potentially the murder weapon. That's nuts. It never happens like that. Anyone who's watched even ten minutes of Law and Order knows that."

"We've got a job to do, and we're going to be thorough about it," Carter said. "In the meantime, don't leave the house once it starts snowing. It's supposed to be a whiteout tonight. It'll be dangerous."

"It's always dangerous when there's a murderer running around," Eu said.

"You know I bet we could find room in that jail for y'all." Writman nodded at Fran. "That one won't take up much room at all."

"Rude," Eu said.

"We'll be back," Carter said, inclining his head toward the door and giving Writman a look.

"Whatever happened to protect and serve," Eu muttered, closing the door.

CHAPTER FOURTEEN

"Well, what do we do now?" Fran asked, wrapping her hands around a mug of tea and shivering.

"Clearly Grandpa Grange set us up. Which means we now know who the killer is, we just have to figure out how to nail him for the crime. I'm also afraid he's going to try to attack Clarissa again, so we need to get him charged and out of there. She must've seen a clue or witnessed something that he did and he's trying to get rid of her," Fran replied.

"He's got a lot of money and apparently isn't afraid to spend it," Fran warned. "That could be dangerous. He already offed his wife and we're nothing to him."

Eu's eyes brightened as inspiration struck. "That's actually not true. We are something to him. We're women. His weakness is other women. If you go on a date with him, you can probably get some great information from him. Maybe get him to incriminate himself."

"What? Why me?" Fran asked.

"Because you know how to flirt, and I don't." Eu shrugged.

"You'd better learn if you ever want Michael to ask you out."

"Like that would ever happen. But focus, you could put your phone on record and have dinner with him. Get him to confess by like, sympathizing with him or something, and we can take the recording to the police."

"That might work." Fran nodded. "But what if he drags me off somewhere and kills me? He may realize we're setting him up because he called the police and tried to frame us."

"That's not likely. He's an old man. He didn't kill his wife with force, he poisoned her," Eu pointed out. "And as far as the pen goes, you could confess to it."

"How can I confess to something that we both know I didn't do?" Fran asked.

"Well, he can't exactly admit that he knows you didn't do it without implicating himself, so he won't have any choice but to play along."

"Yeah, I suppose. But he was strong enough that he tried to strangle his granddaughter," Fran said.

"And he didn't succeed. As far as the poison, definitely make sure that you keep your eyes on your food and drink the whole time. Don't leave the table for even an instant."

"So, this is going to be a thing? I'm really going to go to dinner and flirt with a killer who tried to frame me for his crime. Fran gave Eu a pointed look.

"It may be the only way we can save Clarissa's life and get him in jail," Eu replied

Fran sighed. "Fine, but how do we go about it?"

"You go over and apologize." Eu shrugged.

Fran's brows rose. "Apologize? In his house, where he could kill me, and no one would ever know?"

Eu frowned. “Good point. I’ll have to go with you. Here’s what we’ll do. I’ll text Clarissa and tell her that we’d like to come over again, because we feel bad about leaving before she got off the phone. We’ll go over, I’ll hang out with Clarissa so that I can warn her, and you go flirt with Bernie and offer to take him to dinner to make it up to him.”

“Wait, now I have to buy the killer dinner?” Fran’s mouth dropped open.

“Oh, please. He’s an older southern guy. There’s no way in the world he’d actually allow you to treat. He’ll offer to pay. He may be a murderer, but he still has manners.”

“Good. I’ll order surf and turf, with a beluga caviar appetizer,” Fran replied sourly.

“Good luck finding a place around here that has that kind of food,” Eu commented.

“I know just who to text to ask.” Fran grinned.

“Oh, my goodness, you’ll use any excuse to text Benz, won’t you?” Eu teased.

“Yes ma’am. He’s adorable.”

"Well, okay then, we have a plan. Let me text Clarissa and we'll get it in motion."

CHAPTER FIFTEEN

"Okay, I told Clarissa that we'd come over and hang out around two," Eu told Fran. "She apologized for the phone call and she said that she has a friend going through a bad breakup. Now, as far as our plan, you can practice recording the dinner convo you're going to have with Bernie by having your phone record the conversation when you talk to him today."

Fran took a big breath and blew it out. "But won't it seem like we're setting a trap for him if we have the recording from today?" she asked.

Eu blinked at her for a moment. "Not if we erase it."

"Oh. Right. Good point," Fran agreed, pacing.

"I can't believe that I actually have to say this to you, Ms. Social Butterfly, but don't be nervous. Just be yourself," Eu advised.

Fran stopped pacing and stared at her best friend as though she'd suddenly grown horns. "Be myself. While flirting with a man who murdered his wife and tried to murder his granddaughter. Sure, no problem."

"I believe in you. You've probably flirted with serial killers before and never knew it. How did your call with Benz go?" Eu changed the subject to something that would make her bestie smile.

"Oh, my gosh, girl! It went so well." Fran smiled dreamily. "He recommended The Chateau and said he'd love to take me there sometime. I told him I'd love to make that happen and he wants to go before I leave for home."

"Well check you out. Making arrangements to go on a date with a killer got you a date with the man of your dreams," Eu teased.

"Yeah, if I'm still around to go." Fran gave her a look.

"You will be. Wanna go fishing?"

"More than anything," Fran said dryly.

"Good, let's bundle up."

"Can we at least have another cup of coffee before we go out into the great white north? The snow must be at least a foot deep out there," Fran complained.

"I can do even better than that." Eu grinned. "We'll take a whole thermos of coffee with us, along with some nice warm brownies."

"Okay, now you're talking. Let's make sure to bring enough for Callie, in case she's out there."

"Do I have to?" Eu muttered.

Fran crossed her arms and tapped her foot. "Yes. If you want to get her to open up, eating and drinking coffee in front of her without offering any on the day after a blizzard isn't going to be your best bet."

"Ugh. Fine." Eu sighed.

They trudged through the snow in Eu's front yard and were thrilled to see that the path down to the marina had been cleared, the fishing hole had been cleared and Callie had a space heater sitting on an upside down crate, warming the area around the fishing hole.

"Good morning," they said in unison.

Callie ignored Eu, but nodded at Fran, who wasted no time going over to bring her some coffee and a brownie. They'd thought ahead and had brought mugs and paper plates with them.

Callie had on fingerless gloves and when she reached for the brownie, Fran saw something that made her eyes go wide with what looked like surprise. Eu frowned, not understanding the look and Fran gave a nearly imperceptible shake of her head. Eu shrugged. Fran could tell her about it when they left, whatever it was.

Making herself right at home, Fran sat on an upside down five gallon bucket that she pulled next to Callie's folding chair to have a little chat. Eu ignored them and focused on her fishing, tuning out her bestie's chatter and Callie's muffled responses.

The tip of her pole dipped suddenly, and Eu set her coffee down so abruptly that it spilled onto her glove, soaking through. She reeled with all of her might as Fran grabbed the net and stood beside her, ready to haul in whatever had taken her line so forcefully.

"Oh! I saw it! The color is so pretty," Fran exclaimed, her knees resting against the railing around the fishing hole as she watched for the fish to surface again.

She didn't have long to wait, and as Eu's muscles strained to keep the tip of her pole elevated, Fran scooped up her nice-sized catfish.

"Wow, it's so big," Fran marveled.

"It's definitely a keeper," Eu replied. "Since it's so cold out, I think I'll go clean it now and we can head back up to the cabin."

She went to the cleaning station, running hot water to keep her hands from freezing as she cleaned and fileted the catfish the way that Benz had taught her. She saw Fran talking to Callie, but couldn't hear what either one of them was saying. When she sealed the filets in one of the plastic bags that she always kept handy, she went back to the fishing hole, picked up the thermos and the rest of the brownies. Glancing over at Fran, she inclined her head toward the door. Fran took Callie's empty cup and plate and hurried out behind Eu.

As soon as they were out of earshot, Fran spoke.

"Oh, my gosh, Eu! Did you see Callie's bracelet?" she gasped.

"Callie wears jewelry?" Eu said. "That's something I wouldn't have expected."

"But that's not the point at all," Fran replied, grabbing Eu's arm. "The bracelet was leather, and it had the same pattern on it as your dad's belt. Your mom had to have made it for her."

Eu stopped walking and stared at Fran. "My mother gave Callie a bracelet, and she still wears it? There's no way that's a coincidence." She frowned, thinking. "You have to see if you can find out how that came about and why, if she's still wearing it, she's so hateful toward me."

"Don't you think it would be better if you found that out yourself?" Fran said gently.

Eu sighed and started walking again. "Hard to do when she turns to stone the moment she sees me. Anyway, I'm going to shower so I don't smell like catfish, and then we can eat a little bit of lunch before we head to Farnsworth to put our plan in motion."

"You like this detective stuff, don't you?" Fran asked, smiling and shaking her head.

"I'd like it a whole heckuva lot better if it wasn't always because I was trying to save my own neck…or yours," Eu replied.

"Maybe it could be a career option," Fran suggested.

"Not a chance. As soon as all this weird stuff stops happening to me, the closest that I'm going to get to murder is writing about true crime pieces in an article or two," Eu insisted.

"Uh-huh. I'll believe that when I see it."

"It's true. This cloak and dagger stuff is way too stressful for me. I just want it to be over, once and for all."

"And then what?" Fran asked.

"And then I figure my life out."

CHAPTER SIXTEEN

"Well, here goes nothing. If we fail at this, we're going to have to come up with a whole new strategy," Fran said when they pulled up in front of the Grange mansion.

"We won't fail. Just charm the socks off of a cold-blooded killer and we're good to go," Eu said, her heartbeat accelerating at the thought of Fran being in harm's way.

Clarissa opened the door herself this time.

"Oh, thank goodness you're here. I was about to die of boredom," she drawled. "Come on in."

"Look, Clarissa, we're really sorry that we left while you were on the phone. We just didn't know how long you were going to be, and we didn't want to intrude," Eu said.

Clarissa shrugged. "No worries at all. I would have done the same thing."

"And we'd really like to apologize to your grandfather over the little misunderstanding with the pen," Fran said.

"I don't see that there's anything to apologize for, but if it'll make you feel better, go for it. Do you remember how to get to his study, or should I call Maria to take you there?" Clarissa asked.

"I think we'll be able to find it. Up the stairs and to the left, then left again, right?" Eu said.

"You got it. Just come to the rec room after you're done. I'll have Maria make a snack tray for us and I'll meet you there," Clarissa replied. "I'm thinking an air hockey tournament is in order." She grinned.

"You're on!" Fran replied, sounding amazingly calm.

"Hi, Bernie," Fran called out softly, knocking on the doorframe of his study door. "Can we come in?"

"Of course, come in, come in," he beckoned, standing and beaming at them.

Eu and Fran exchanged a look. He seemed awfully glad to see two people that he had reported to the police.

“We wanted to apologize for what happened with your pen,” Fran said.

Bernie frowned. “Huh?”

“Your pen. The silver one that went missing,” Eu prompted.

“Oh, no worries at all. Turns out the police found it,” Bernie said. “I bought that in Paris, you know.”

“How nice,” Eu said, giving Fran a puzzled look. Fran shrugged.

“Would you excuse me? I need to visit the ladies’ room,” Eu said.

“Sure thing, honey. Down the hall and to the right, can’t miss it.” Bernie pointed.

“Thanks so much.”

Eu left and pulled the door almost closed behind her, but instead of going to the bathroom, she stood just outside the door so that she could hear the conversation between Fran and Bernie and make sure that Fran was safe.

"So, I was hoping that maybe I could make it up to you by taking you to dinner," Fran said.

"Make what up to me?" Bernie asked.

"The pen thing, you know."

"Pens go missing sometimes. It happens, but I'll be more than happy to take you to dinner. I'm old fashioned enough that I can't let a lady take me out no matter how beautiful she is." He chuckled.

"Oh, listen to you. You're going to make me blush," Fran replied, laying it on thick.

"You ain't seen nothing yet, honey. It's gonna have to be tonight though," Bernie said.

"Tonight? Why tonight?" Fran asked, managing to sound coquettish.

"Because tomorrow night is Christmas Eve. I have to be here for my granddaughter."

"Oh, right, of course. I totally forgot that tomorrow is Christmas Eve. Well then, it's a date."

Eu heard a noise nearby and tiptoed toward the opposite end of the hall, convinced that Fran was going to be just fine.

CHAPTER SEVENTEEN

"It seemed like he had no clue what we were talking about when we mentioned the pen," Fran said, holding up her hair as Eu fastened a necklace around her neck.

"Well, yeah. It's not like he's going to admit that he set you up," Eu replied.

"True. Thank goodness the thrift shop had a decent dress for me to wear to dinner," Fran replied, checking her appearance in the mirror.

"I'd say that dress is borderline indecent, which is perfect for this particular occasion," Eu teased.

"Gee, thanks. Way to make me feel safe and secure." Fran made a face.

"You'll be fine."

"Uh-huh. And what's with your outfit? Why are you all dressed in black? Early mourning?"

"Very funny. I'm going to be lurking around outside the restaurant to make sure that our killer doesn't try anything sketchy," Eu replied.

"Oh, good." Fran let out a sigh of relief.

They heard a rumbling sound outside and hurried from Eu's room.

"Looks like your ride is here," Eu said, peering out of the guest room window at a massive SUV that had pulled up in front of the cabin.

Moments later, a uniformed chauffeur knocked politely on the door and announced that he was there for Fran. When he saw the black patent leather pumps that she was wearing, he asked if he could assist her to the car. When Fran said yes, he swung her up into his arms and carried her to the SUV, gently placing her on the backseat. She waggled her eyebrows over his shoulder, making Eu giggle, even as nervous as she was.

As soon as the SUV was out of sight, Eu raced to Michael's car, hoping that it could make it up the hill if she followed the SUV's tracks.

"It's weird that they plowed last time it snowed, but not this time," she murmured, a pit of dread forming in her stomach. If she couldn't make it up the hill and get to The Chateau, Fran would be on her own with someone who had already killed once and had attempted another murder. "Hopefully those videos I looked up on how to make it up a snowy hill were correct."

She nearly got stuck at the top of the hill, but managed to slide out onto the highway, where conditions weren't ideal, but were much better than the parking lot had been. She spotted the SUV ahead and hung back a safe distance, so that she wouldn't be seen.

When the SUV turned into the drop-off lane for The Chateau, Eu continued on and parked in the furthest corner of the lot, where she wouldn't be seen. There was a limousine in front of the entrance, and Bernard got out of it as the SUV pulled up behind it.

"Well, at least she didn't have to ride with him to the restaurant," Eu murmured, watching as Bernard kissed Fran's hand and led her into the restaurant, his hand in the small of her back. She felt acid rising in the back of her throat and opened the car door, drinking in fresh icy air as she darted around the side of the restaurant and made a beeline for the forest behind it.

Using the tall trees as cover in the pale moonlight, Eu trudged through the snow, keeping an eye on the back windows of the restaurant, thanking her lucky stars when she saw Fran and Bernie being seated at a table for two right next to one of the windows.

As she crept closer to the front of the tree line, Eu saw a slight movement ahead and heard a faint clicking sound. Her heart in her throat, she slowly moved closer, keeping an eye on Fran at the same time.

As she got closer to the clicking sound, a dark figure suddenly stood up, startling the daylights out of her.

"Eu?" A familiar voice reached out of the darkness.

"Clarissa?" Eu said, relieved. They both laughed.

"What are you doing here?" Eu asked, trotting as quickly as she could through the snow.

"Taking photos of my grandpa. I used to document his affairs in case any of the women tried to file charges or something weird, but now I just love seeing the joy on his face. That's your friend Fran, isn't it?" Clarissa asked, snapping another photo.

"Yeah, she has a thing for older guys." Eu shrugged, crossing her fingers inside her coat pocket. She didn't like lying to Clarissa, but she didn't want to compromise Fran either. Bernie's granddaughter might not appreciate the two of them setting him up to be busted for murder.

"Well that definitely works for my grandpa. As long as she doesn't break his heart."

"She's not the heartbreaker type," Eu assured her. At least that part was true.

"Wait, why are you here?" Clarissa asked.

"I always keep an eye on Fran whenever she's out with a new guy," Eu replied, astonished at how easy it was becoming to fib her way out of situations. It made her feel icky, as though she needed a shower.

"Seems a bit obsessive, but I get it, I guess. Wait, this doesn't have anything to do with an off the wall theory about him being a killer, does it?" Clarissa asked.

"Seriously? Do you think I'd let my best friend have dinner with a killer?"

"Fair point," Clarissa conceded. "Man, it's cold out here. I think I'm going to call it a day after a few more shots. Wanna go somewhere for food that doesn't have mortgage-sized menu prices?" she asked.

Eu panicked briefly but kept her expression neutral. There was no way in the world she was leaving Fran unattended with a killer. "Maybe in a few. That's a great looking camera you have. Do you mind if I have a look? I don't know much about them, but my dad used to collect cameras."

"He doesn't anymore?" Clarissa asked, handing over the camera while still watching her grandfather.

"He passed a few years ago." Eu subtly turned the camera away from Clarissa so that she could scroll through recent photos.

"Aw, I'm sorry. Were you close?"

Eu fought to pay attention while she quickly scanned the photos.

"Yeah, very. My mom dumped me on him right after I was born, so he was all I had."

"I hear ya. My grandpa and my real grandma raised me. My grandma was the best. She passed four years ago, and he married Gabby about a year later."

"And now she's gone, too," Eu said, affecting a sympathetic tone. "Did you get along with her? It must've been hard adapting when she came along."

"Yeah, she was great at home. I think she was just really nervous in public and showed it by being loud and obnoxious," Clarissa chuckled, her expression wistful.

Swallowing hard, Eu fought to contain her reaction at the series of photos that she'd just seen. She quickly switched out of viewing mode and handed the camera back. "Yep, yours looks just like one of the ones my dad had, but his was way older I think. Yours has so many buttons I wouldn't know what to do with it."

"Yeah?" Clarissa said, flicking the mode switch. "You certainly managed to navigate through my photos easily enough." She glanced down at the display.

"And just when I thought we could be friends, and I wouldn't have to kill you. My grandfather was supposed to be next, but now you've moved up to his spot." She reached into a pocket on the inside of her coat.

"Kill me?" Eu said loudly, hoping that she might attract someone's attention if sound carried over snow. "Why, because I saw the photos you took of you with the poison, putting it into your grandmother's wine? And the photos of the inside of my house when you came in and mussed things up just to mess with my head? And the photos of you putting your grandfather's pen in Fran's coat pocket while we were on the house tour with him? Those photos? You thought you were so smart. Setting up the new girl in town," Eu babbled, trying to buy herself some time to think.

Clarissa had something in her hand when she withdrew it from her inner coat pocket, something that glinted in the moonlight.

Seeing no other choice, Eu followed her instincts and launched herself at Clarissa, who fell back into the snow upon impact, a knife flashing in her hand.

She slashed at Eu, slicing through her thrift store coat and grazing her upper arm before Eu plopped down on her chest and secured Clarissa's arms under her knees. White-hot pain shot like lightning through Eu's arm, but she held the killer's wrists down in the snow, knowing she didn't dare let her go.

"You're next," Clarissa hissed, through clenched teeth. "You're going down, Eugenia."

"Somehow I don't think so," a familiar voice drawled. Eu glanced over her shoulder and saw Benz, Carter, Writman, and two other deputies coming out of the tree line.

"When Fran told me about your cockamamy scheme, I had to come see it for myself, and bring some of my good buddies with me," Benz said as the men jogged through calf-deep snow toward them.

With an unearthly grunt, Clarissa bucked Eu off of her. Eu flew to the side, landing on her injured arm. She cried out in pain, but when Clarissa tried to run, she lunged and grabbed the killer's ankle, making her faceplant in the snow.

"Wow, that looked like it hurt," Carter observed mildly, dropping to his knees beside Clarissa, handcuffs in his hand.

He planted a knee in the killer's back and Writman unslung her camera, taking it into evidence.

CHAPTER EIGHTEEN

Fran and Eu sat on the couch, dressed in festive Christmas sweaters, drinking cocoa, eating cookies they'd made, and watching the sappiest Christmas movies that they could find.

"I'm so glad we got all that murder nastiness out of the way before Christmas Eve," Fran said. "But I really do feel bad for Bernie. He was probably devastated when he found out that Clarissa is the one who killed his wife and that he was next on the list. He thought the sun rose and set in that girl."

"Yeah, she had us all fooled," Eu agreed.

"And surprisingly, he actually wasn't nearly as creepy as I thought he'd be. He was a flirt, yes, but he was also a perfect gentleman and seemed harmless," Fran said. "I've had much worse dates with guys my own age."

"At least you got some free lobster out of it." Eu laughed. "We also lucked out that they matched her fingerprints on the pen and vial that she slipped into your coat pocket."

"It's a Christmas miracle." Fran chuckled, holding up her mug. Eu clinked hers against it.

A knock sounded at the door, and they stared at each other.

"You've gotta be kidding me," Eu muttered. "What could they possibly want now?"

She yanked open the door and saw Callie, holding a present wrapped in brown paper that was secured with a bow made of twine.

"Merry Christmas," Eu said, not knowing what to do next.

"Merry Christmas," Callie replied, handing Eu the present. "I'm sorry for being rude."

Eu nodded, speechless. Fran joined her at the door and her eyes went wide.

"Uh, would you like to come in and have some cocoa and cookies?" Fran asked, as Eu stood, dumbstruck.

"No. Gotta get home. Just wanted to say Merry Christmas," Callie replied.

"Thank you so much," Eu finally found her voice. "Can we at least give you some brownies to take with you?"

"Wouldn't mind that." Callie nodded.

"Do you want to come in while I wrap them up?" Eu asked.

"Nope."

"Okay, I'll be right back," Eu replied, nonplussed, leaving Fran to keep their unexpected visitor company as she stood on the porch.

Eu hurriedly wrapped up the rest of the brownies that she'd warmed up and gave them to Callie.

"Thanks," Callie said simply, before turning and trudging back through the snow toward her cabin.

Fran looked utterly flabbergasted when she turned to Eu, taking her by the shoulders.

"Oh my gosh, Eu. I know two things about Callie now."

"Oh? Do tell," Eu said, still reeling from the encounter herself.

"First, she was a model. I've seen surfing posters with her face on them, that's why she looks so familiar. No wonder she loves it when I talk about my surf shop. It all makes sense now."

Eu's mouth dropped open. "Really? How can you tell it's her? No offense, but she doesn't look like a model."

Fran smiled a Cheshire-cat smile. "No, but her daughter does."

"Daughter? What on earth are you talking about? Did you put peppermint schnapps in your cocoa?" Eu's brows rose.

"No, but you might want to once I show you something," Fran replied. "Go get your laptop."

Fran tapped away at the keyboard looking up vintage surfing ads and showed the one she'd been talking about to Eu. Eu's heart leapt to her throat.

“Now tell me, who does that look exactly like?” Fran asked.

“Well, it looks a lot like a much younger version of Callie, but it looks exactly like… Clarissa. Clarissa is Callie’s daughter? I thought her parents died in a crash or something. I wonder if Callie knows that her daughter is on her way to jail for murder,” Eu said, shaking her head.

“If she gets any kind of local news, she probably saw Clarissa’s picture and realized it. There’s gotta be more to that story,” Fran said. “I wonder if Clarissa knows that her mother is alive.”

Eu nodded. “That’s definitely a conversation for another day. Wow, I can’t believe it… Callie, a model, who would’ve thought it?”

“I keep telling you, things aren’t always as they seem.”

After switching from cocoa to wine and popping a massive bowl of popcorn, the besties went back to watching movies, but it wasn’t very long before there was another knock at the door.

Eu glanced at her phone to check the time. “It’s kinda late, but maybe Callie changed her mind and wants to join us after all.” She shrugged.

She went to the door and blushed from the tips of her toes to the roots of her hair when she saw Michael wearing a Santa hat, carrying a big sack of gifts, and a basket of something that smelled beyond delicious.

“Merry Christmas, Eugenia,” he said, putting down the sack of gifts and wrapping her in a one-armed hug.

“Oh, my gosh. Santa brought Eu a hot professor for Christmas,” Fran blurted, making them all crack up. Michael gave her a hug and Eu invited him in.

“Do I smell popcorn?” he asked.

“There’s plenty. And we’ve moved from cocoa to wine if that’s good with you. We’re watching Christmas movies,” Eu said, entirely unable to keep a big silly grin from her face.

“Perfect. Where should I put the presents?” Michael asked.

“What presents?” Fran asked, peeking into the bag.

"I brought presents for both of you because I knew you'd never leave your bestie alone for the holiday, Fran." He grinned.

"You got that right. Oh, my goodness. It's university swag!" Fran exclaimed with delight.

"Yep. All warm things, too. Sweatshirts, scarves, mittens, and fuzzy blankets. I also brought some things that I baked when I got in this afternoon." He held up the basket.

"Well, in all the craziness, we forgot to put up a tree, so we just stacked ours by the fireplace," Eu said.

"What are we watching?" Michael asked, as they all settled in on the couch, with Fran on Eu's left, Michael on Eu's right, and the giant popcorn bowl on Eu's lap.

"Sappy Christmas movies," Fran replied. "So how long are you visiting?"

"Great, I love sappy Christmas movies. I'll be around for a few days or so," Michael replied, making Eu's pulse flutter.

"Oh good, so there'll be fresh muffins for Christmas morning," Fran teased.

"I'll happily make them." Michael grinned.

"I'll cook bacon," Eu volunteered.

"What more could anyone want?" Fran said.

"What more indeed?" Michael said lightly, with a smile that was just for Eu.

***

If you enjoyed Baited Breath, check out The Reel Truth, book 4 in the Fish Camp Cozy Mystery series.

ALSO BY SUMMER PRESCOTT

Check out all the books in Summer Prescott's catalog!

Summer Prescott Book Catalog

AUTHOR'S NOTE

I'd love to hear your thoughts on my books, the storylines, and anything else that you'd like to comment on—reader feedback is very important to me. My contact information, along with some other helpful links, is listed on the next page. If you'd like to be on my list of "folks to contact" with updates, release and sales notifications, etc.… just shoot me an email and let me know. Thanks for reading!

Also…

… if you're looking for more great reads, Summer Prescott Books publishes several popular series by outstanding Cozy Mystery authors.

CONTACT SUMMER PRESCOTT BOOKS PUBLISHING

Twitter: @summerprescott1

Bookbub: https://www.bookbub.com/authors/summer-prescott

Blog and Book Catalog: http://summerprescottbooks.com

Email: summer.prescott.cozies@gmail.com

YouTube: https://www.youtube.com/channel/UCngKNUkDdWuQ5k7-Vkfrp6A

And…be sure to check out the Summer Prescott Cozy Mysteries fan page and Summer Prescott Books Publishing Page on Facebook – let's be friends!

To download a free book, and sign up for our fun and exciting newsletter, which will give you opportunities to win prizes and swag, enter contests, and be the first to know about New Releases, click here: http://summerprescottbooks.com

Printed in Great Britain
by Amazon

59926538R10092